Pleasure

ALSO BY NTHIKENG MOHLELE

Rusty Bell (2014)

'*Rusty Bell* is an intricate exploration of love, fate, lust, death and grief … illustrating that the light is not the place for answers, because sometimes they are visible only from the shadows.' – Lloyd Gedye, *The Con*

'*Rusty Bell* grapples with a large range of issues presented to the reader in lyrical prose. And this is where [Nthikeng] differs from his peers because, for me, many South African authors write conceptually interesting novels, but often at the expense of literariness. Nthikeng, however, can't be faulted at the level of the sentence … *Rusty Bell* is a subtly crafted novel with a philosophical complexity that, at any given point, is poised for lines of flight.' – Chantelle Gray van Heerden, *SLiP*

Small Things (2013)

'Behind this story of love, music and the eternal quest lies an artistic sensibility as generous as it is complex. The prose is rich in texture, the final effect melancholy and comic in equal proportions.' – JM Coetzee

'*Small Things* is a tribute to the push back of the will to exist with dignity against the callous forces of a society that, in its haste to move on from a terrible past, has left many of its (unacknowledged) struggle heroes unhomed and rudderless. In that sense it is an extended thought experiment: how does one attain freedom after emancipation, if the withdrawal of overt oppression is the first step on the journey to freedom?' – Joshua Maserow, *Aerodrome*

The Scent of Bliss (2008)

'An outstanding poetic piece of work … Mohlele's voice is novel and shows a concern … for beautiful language for its own sake.'
– Percy Zvomuya, *Mail & Guardian*

'An assured debut by a writer who wields his pen with flair and confidence.' – Arja Salafranca, *The Star Tonight*

Pleasure

Nthikeng Mohlele

PICADOR AFRICA

First published in 2016 by Picador Africa
an imprint of Pan Macmillan South Africa
Private Bag X19, Northlands
Johannesburg, 2116

www.panmacmillan.co.za

ISBN 978-1-77010-485-3
eBook ISBN 978-1-77010-486-0

© 2016 Nthikeng Mohlele

All rights reserved. No part of this publication may be reproduced, stored in or introduced into a retrieval system, or transmitted, in any form, or by any means (electronic, mechanical, photocopying, recording or otherwise), without the prior written permission of the publisher. Any person who does any unauthorised act in relation to this publication may be liable to criminal prosecution and civil claims for damages.

This book is a work of fiction. Any resemblance to actual places or persons, living or dead, is purely coincidental.

Editing by Sean Fraser
Proofreading by Kelly Norwood-Young
Design and typesetting by Fire and Lion
Cover design by K4
Cover photograph by Allen Jenkins/Trevillion Images
Author photograph by Oupa Nkosi, courtesy of the *Mail & Guardian*

Printed and bound by Novus Print Solution

In celebration and appreciation of my wife, Sharon Mohlele – formerly Morokolo – from 'Bugaboo' with an educated heart; son and friend, Miles Mohlele, from 'Mister' with love; and niece Maya 'Angelou', my brother and confidant Jeffrey's lovely little human.

Author's Note

Pleasure is a work of fiction – fiction that draws from, reflects on and dramatises a period in history, its personalities and events, without being constrained by them. The intention of this novel is not to reproduce history or place; it is, rather, a narrative that takes artistic liberties with its depiction of the history from which it draws. No attempt has been made to follow to the letter the unfolding of actual events in a period that has already been painstakingly documented.

Nthikeng Mohlele
Johannesburg, South Africa
March 2016

'Most men pursue pleasure with such breathless haste that they hurry past it.'

– Søren Kierkegaard

The Dreamer in the Bathtub

I had, in the noisiest and most uncomfortable of beds in my late father's Casablanca Estates apartment overlooking the sea, furnace-hot intercourse – of the mind and later of the body – with one Abella Beaudrie, a gorgeous visiting professor. My life is a concoction of humanitarian yearnings, artistic preoccupations, an avid collection of souvenirs, occasionally of the brassiere kind; an eternal death, dying in endless reincarnations – some deaths simple, others elaborate. After many false starts, detours, harrowing omissions, I still cannot tell for sure what, in the realm of pleasure, must be understood. Most men – not all, of course – welcome an opportunity to be pleasured by a woman. Not solely for the pleasure (because this can never be guaranteed, and there are tales of unintended consequences: a missed appointment, a sudden period, bodies stripped of clothes, their imperfections laid bare, becoming impenetrable fortresses), but for the possibilities that pleasure is able to birth: laughter, shared secrets, grave confessions.

Because pleasure is an occupation of mind, body and soul, it seems to me impossible to place burdens of proof on something so elusive – which forces me to focus on something equally deceptive yet present in both thought and action. I think of pleasure as a slave to the *imagination*. It can, at the whim of the imagination, be either passive or delayed. When delayed, reserved for appropriate moments, for answers from would-be companions in courtship, the very existence of unconfirmed possibilities can itself be pleasurable: something as mundane as observing a stranger skilfully eat pasta, for instance.

Pleasure's glow, its very essence, remains experienced and yet not fully comprehended. It seems to me that all of life is one long quest: an attempt to own pleasure, imprison it, distort or bend it to breaking point, to invent and birth its new variations. Even pleasures of the brutal kind, those that mark and chew and deform. The problem with pleasure – whether experienced, sought or imagined – is the sheer scale of it, its variations, the endlessness of it all. Be it admiration for an aesthetically pleasing human form or the sensation of sleep, the itch of a healing wound, the mental image of a bowl of strawberries or moist breasts, a lone penetrating voice that rises and falls during those mass choir toils, the warm and sustained applause that follows, or Professor Beaudrie ending her lectures on 'Sexuality and Modern Societies' at the Culture Institute with a considered and delicious: *Donc, il paraît que l'érotisme restera très longtemps avec l'être humain* – So, it seems the erotic will be with humans for a very long time to come.

Abella says, in the privacy of our noisy bed, 'Thank you, universe, for all things lascivious.' *Merci, l'univers, pour tout ce qui est lascif.* Charming linguistic registers, the French language. Pleasurable. Like Sepedi, which when spoken equates to licking and biting into sweet plums, being tickled with a feather down the spine. Maybe that is what must be understood: that life should be both lived *and* imagined. Like the long-abandoned French villas I imagine Abella exploring, this middle-aged, sensual academic with erotic sensibilities who would still be beautiful even if she answered to Babineaux or Blanchett, Monet or Paquet. It is amusing that pleasure continues to prance and dance around me without the slightest disquiet: children worshipping their ice-cream cones at the boardwalk, the jewelled birds that frequent my pot plants for unknown reasons, the satisfying trickery of a sudden sneeze, the aroma of coffee brewing in offices brimming with thoughts and laughter, beautiful women wrestling errant umbrellas and summer dresses in rainy gusts. The pleasures of a humid evening on a restaurant deck, kiss-related contentment of strangers, delights brought about by private thoughts, the satisfaction of yawning and crackling bones after a long sleep.

There are also perverse pleasures, pleasures savoured in concealment. It is when the concealment fails, or the betrayal of that concealment – which is not the same as it failing, that dungeon doors are locked, that the afflictions of conscience emerge. I repeat: the totality of existence seems to me to be the pursuit of pleasure; from the mundane to the mesmeric, from the mesmeric to the weighty, which are but stepping stones to far more rare and precarious pleasures. The higher one climbs the pleasure ladder, the heavier the burdens of conscience – which is understandable, but still without remedy.

My official documents state my names as Milton Moremi Mohlele, though I am known simply as Milton. I am studious, a literary slut of sorts: solitary, cerebral, mysterious. And divorced. Some ladies, even the most reserved ones, gather courage to compliment my quiet nature and, on occasions but very rarely, wake up in my bed, prance to the bathroom in the nude, curious but content: Alexis, Abella, Masechaba visit, bearing gifts, their hearts on fire.

I am older now – wiser, I suppose, more philosophical about nocturnal feminine giggles. I have kissed a lot of women in my life, filling in a mental kissing register with patience and panache until the last of the beautiful women is charmed, cornered, caressed, kissed. Many want to offer much more, but I politely decline, to their utter frustration and bewilderment. Kisses are safe preoccupations and, if properly practised, manageable. They have the potential to illuminate hearts without dimming the imagination, which once properly cultivated is a source of unparalleled and limitless pleasure. I am not a womaniser, not in the truest sense. What is womanising, anyway? Is it the crude pursuit of rudimentary lusts or something much more vulnerable: a burning desire to belong? Is it a science of sorts that establishes and discards rules as and when convenient? Is it in its truest sense an elusive charm, a craft at once detested but somehow tolerated, sought, envied even?

I am neither loved nor universally admired, but I am, within the confines of my profession and track record, respected. I enjoy a modest but weighty fame: television appearances, me discussing all manner of things – ranging from goings-on in the theatre circuit, a drop in film standards, illiterate book reviewers. But mine is a dry kind of fame: a quick nod my way from complete strangers, a hesitant wave of the hand, conspiratorial nudges from passing lovers; it is a bland fame, unlike that reserved for rock stars in leather pants, the kind that urges throngs to erupt into stampedes and succumb to uncontrollable heart palpitations, panty throwing and fainting spells.

I notice things. Even the smallest, most insignificant of them: colour contrasts on the buttons of a blouse, dust particles settling on gravestones. I notice shadows in magazine images, rust in the inner workings of jumbo-jet wings, steam shot from boiling kettles and suddenly dissipating into nothingness, the varying shapes of sugar granules, the faint nerves on my lovers' eyeballs. I take note of toothbrush designs, colour combinations, toothpaste residue hiding between the brush fibres; I pay attention to the curvature of moon phases, idle tomatoes changing complexion from salmon to blood red, Abella's pubic hair coloured a rusty brown by urine and time. I observe the wing patterns on murdered mosquitoes, raindrops on the patio tiles, the wheezing sounds made by babies sucking on emptying bottles, low-decibel groans of mattress springs when I cannot sleep, the wind sweeping prayers from the mosque on Twelfth Avenue. I notice fat-content readings on food labels, thread counts and symmetry on tablecloths. I dream the most daring and colourful of dreams, the interpretations of which may occupy me for weeks if not months on end. It is perhaps true to say that I admire my dreams, that I am at times unsettled by them, and have a fear that one day they will vanish, simply dry up. I don't know why this is so. I have, in the absence of a convincing answer, simply submitted to the most logical of stances: that some dreams are more colourful than others.

I have a brother, Bull, younger by eleven years, who has for some reason never found it important to lead a respectable life. Both my parents are late, of natural causes (kidney failure, heartbreak), and rest at the Melrose Cemetery, where I seldom visit, but when I do I do so in the company of Milton and Rilke. I drive Father's cream 1984 Mercedes, lacking in the luminance associated with pricier vehicles, am a practising vegetarian, a lover of goat's milk, and keen observer of women in various stages of anger or arousal. If you had asked me, when I was eight or nine, what I wanted to be when grown, I would without hesitation have said, 'A policeman.' I have, even from that tender age, found the concept of handcuffs fascinating – how the accused surrenders all individuality, wrists cuffed behind his back, overwhelmed by the machinations of justice. In my imagination, the accused were – strangely – always men; it never occurred to me that women could commit crimes. But, apart from reading English and German poets in graveyards, I cannot say I have any other eccentricities. Perhaps I do, and they have simply not been pointed out to me, or are not prominent enough to warrant attention.

I sit on the balcony of the Culture Institute, thinking. A bird perches on a rose bush. It is not a big bird, sized for beauty and brisk movements, a lonesome birdsong at once vulnerable and soothing: throaty chuckles that sound like teaspoons tumbling into a puddle. It is a beautiful creature, mostly yellow, with dashes of deep red and blue speckles. The balcony overlooks the Redeemed Church of God, whose creed claims that 'Jesus Christ is the same, yesterday, today and forever'. Even the divine have limitations, I think. A monotony, a sameness, implied boredom. I find this terrifying, but unfathomable. Maybe it means that He, Jesus, is reliable, and that's not such a bad thing. I am not like Him, though. I don't feel qualified to speculate about forever, but I know for sure that I have never been the same: yesterday or today. Even the birds that visit the garden, that hover among the flowers, are not the same. They also don't come for the same reasons. This one, prancing about on toothpick-sized legs, loves the sunflowers, feels entitled to the pollen on most afternoons. But there are others. Worm hunters. Thirsty wanderers. Concert convenors. Lonely bachelors. Attention seekers.

Trouble loves me. That's for sure. My life has been composed of me side-stepping all sorts of troubles, ones I was born with (my temperament, idealism) and those I found in the universe. It is as if they seek me out, can smell me, like a bear sniffs victims at great distances, then follows a trail, claws at the ready, to do battle. It feels to me that I will always exist in my father's shadow, his fame, that I will never make much of anything of weight and substance, that I will always skirt soiling my hands, never quite get to the centre of the flame.

That I have my father's name is rewarding, but also a yoke. When will all these comparisons end? I cannot help but feel that I will never measure up in all sorts of other things too. Money. Crystal thoughts. The adoration of women. Even my affairs, though I am unmarried, are tentative and guarded, never quite fill me with passion and contentment. There is, even at their most intricate, always something missing, a feeling that something is deformed, overvalued, or even unimportant. My lovers do not know this, of course; they might sense the odd, momentary hesitation, but the greater void I save for myself. I soak in long foamy baths with wine by my side, accompanied by Father's rare jazz recordings. I deny the water freedom to cool, to get cold, by pouring hot water whenever the slightest change of temperature is detected. Reading in the bath has its perks: solitude, a freshness, elusive lucidity not easily attained in other living spaces.

I am a handsome man: not bony, not fat, of the sought-after height, and one who, as scores of ladies have remarked, if not confessed, has the most beautiful and reassuring hands, hands that have touched them, led them, comforted and grabbed them, guided them, undressed them, explored them, and – jealous and enraged – almost slapped one. There is a complexity in love, of course, but that's for optimists, for there exists in practical living a certain caution that commits the heart to certain forms of blindness. Hesitation. Self-pity. Despair.

I have my foibles too.

There are times, for instance, when I miss smoking, that protracted suicide, when I miss the thoughtlessness of it all, ruining lungs with measured gestures, timed self-destruction. I admit that listening to Billie or Miles or Coltrane is not quite the same without the cigarette smoke curling mid-air, blue and determined, like waves from the brush of a drunk painter, like mock clouds.

I will never be like my father: too much talent, a disruptive temperament. Everybody reads him, some illiterate snobs lie about reading him, bookstores stock him en masse. He is sure to keep translators busy for the next hundred years. I read him too, even reread him, with admiration, jealousy and detached bitterness, and try my utmost to trace his style, his feelings, the manner of his omissions. That he is dead does not help, but even if he were alive, I know I would not have got answers to my rather oblique questions about writing: how does one know when a theme is worth pursuing? And once that is established, how does one balance heart and mind in performing autopsies on the theme, and – if he was in the mood to talk – how does a writer conceal himself and yet gainfully mine himself for things profound? Dreams, for instance. If I were to write about my dreams, what would be the themes, the spark? Would it be war, love, death, suffering, or would it be pleasure with a capital *P*? And, if it were *Pleasure*, where would it begin and end, in real life or in my dreams? If one of my lovers, because I had been tossing and turning in my sleep, asks what I had dreamt, what would I say? That I desire other women, women who occasionally grace my dreams? It's like being entombed in ice, these questions, this probing about literature, about the universe. And if my dreams come to steer me towards pleasure as a possible theme, why are they so confused, so contradictory?

The only time Father ever raised his head from his Remington 5, eyes misty with tears, the only time he said something directly about literature, in those washed-out pyjamas of his, was: 'Writing is not an act of creation but of *feeling*. You cannot create that which is not felt.' He continued assaulting his typewriter into the early hours, a constant strangling of the keys, at once fluid, musical even, so habitual I could tell when he hit a wall, when a thought escaped expression, when he finally pinned it to the wall, set his Remington firing squad at it, punched holes in it, maimed it, then nursed it back to health. Book after book he bled out, set fire to lives, drowned himself in coffee and bananas, thus nullifying my chances of ever being anything resembling a true writer. I have read those reviews: 'spell-binding, profound, rare' and suchlike. What am I, of the daring dreams, expected to feel, to create?

I have had my moments of utter joy witnessing my father so revered, so exalted, of passive envy at seeing him soar, moments of grief at losing him. I turn down countless invitations by universities, stale book festivals, radio stations and television networks, invitations to speak, to reflect on my father. What more is there to say other than that the man was brilliant and is deceased? Why am I being mocked, scrutinised, expected to resurrect the dead? Isn't every literary journal swarming with at least three essays on him, reflections whose sole purpose is to worship him? I have my sentimental moments, sitting in his study, the burgundy curtains drawn, the sea humming, the morning light drawing mid-air swords across his desk, that cream jersey of his weighing me down – a note reminding him to phone the Revenue Service still in one of the pockets. I will myself to feed paper into the Remington in the hope that I will ignite some connection, some familiarity, however distant, with his way with words, that mind of his that could cut through steel. But the chair is uncomfortable, the misty view dreary and uninspiring, the keys clunky and without feeling. How was he able to write *A Minute After Midnight*, that flammable masterpiece, while presiding over this view? Or did he not notice the cargo ships that dot the horizon, their rusty sides crisscrossing the sea by day, the momentary flashes of light when lit by helicopters come nightfall? Was there something in this view that became embedded in one's very bones? How did such beauty, such warmth, such range in *A Minute After Midnight* come from staring at the sea? What of all these books, stacked shoulder high, these musings on planets, on Judas Iscariot, on necrophilia, even sunflower gardening? And that hair of his that cast shadows on the walls, these Malcolm X glasses behind which bloodshot eyes stared and toiled at the Remington for hours on end without as much as a sip of water.

And Mother? She was, if pictures are anything to go by, unhappy, ageing, with a mute growl. There remained, to the very end, a tinge of longing in her eyes, a distant calculation, of a life disrupted. But that is news for another day, a calmer time.

Alexis

It could be a temporary madness – a momentary surge of feeling – utterly consuming, rare, but intense enough to leave me content and feather light. Today is one of those mornings when the madness pursues me, courts me, pulls faces, sticks out a rude tongue. I once erroneously concluded that that madness was sparked by loneliness, or those unforeseen gusts of euphoric happiness without bounds that often crawl out of nowhere. It turns out it is triggered by all sorts of things: beautiful women, gentle music, even the odd rainbow that momentarily adorns the high heavens – as seen from my hailstone-clean window on the fortieth floor of Casablanca Estates.

Because that feeling, that utter joy, has been so reliable in tickling me in delicate places, I – again – wrongly assume that it will end well, with me floating in a whirlwind of bliss. I am fondling, squeezing, massaging, tapping, and later downright banging the steering wheel to the thunderous groove of 'Thunderstruck', one hand momentarily scratching my ribs in intricate guitar mimes in an effort to contain the charge that bolts me to the seat, oblivious to one incriminating fact: doing 105 in a 60-kilometre-per-hour zone. I almost wipe out an obese traffic officer, all sweat and bulges, his khaki uniform threatening to tear open at any second.

He has a long tooth that breaks rank with the rest, sticks out from between his cracked lips (hunger or the heat?), tasting the air like a snake's tongue. This whale of a man, whose breeches are swallowed back and front by lumpy thighs and a generous spectacle of buttocks, whose bloodshot eyes and furrowed brow confirm dictatorial tendencies, whose gravel face is abused by a blunt razor, whose badge announces him as Bezuidenhout, jumps sideways, just in time to avoid being run over by my ancient but oh-so-fast car.

I plant my foot on the brake, bringing the German thoroughbred to a screeching halt. Officer Bezuidenhout simply stands there, hands on his hips: relieved, annoyed, confrontational. He marshals his parachute of a belly, a bulging sack besieged by sweat and hair peeping through between his shirt buttons, and approaches my window. I expect body odour, but am pleasantly surprised to be met by an inviting scent, musk at first, but layered with a fresh fruity fragrance I cannot quite place. He plants himself alongside my window, impatient and irritable, sarcastic and patronising: 'Why would anyone, seemingly composed and responsible, drive a Mercedes in such a reckless manner? How could you, with your satanic music, sir, blaring for everyone as far as Cairo to hear, drive a Mercedes in such a disgraceful manner?'

I promptly turn down that AC/DC masterpiece, performed and recorded live at River Plate, Buenos Aires, that has swelled my temporary madness to stratospheric heights and answer meekly: 'I am clearly in the wrong, officer, and for that I am truly sorry.'

He looks at me with suspended rage, in disbelief, and counters: 'Clearly in the wrong. Truly sorry. Hmm. Driver's licence?' I hand it to him. He walks around the car, checks the licence disc on the windshield, frowns, shakes his head, returns to my window. He sneezes – five intense sneezes, spraying me with a mist of saliva. I must have shown disdain, but am quick to respond with a restrained 'Bless you', for he wastes no time retaliating.

'Only God can bless me, not you! Your driver's licence expired three months ago. Your car licence four months, twenty-seven days ago. Your windshield is cracked, your tyres smooth as tomatoes, and your bumper paintwork unbecoming of a Mercedes. There is no infringement fine for your kind of offences: attempted murder of a traffic officer, expired licences, blitzing forty-five kilometres over the speed limit, intolerance for an innocent sneeze, that satanic music of yours clearly impairing your senses, driving with no regard for other motorists, and not convincing in your show of remorse!'

I am tongue-tied, and try to offer him more by way of remorse (how does one measure remorse?), but all that does is prompt him to wag a finger in my face: 'Your crimes are many and varied. In this heat, you – even as you face charges of attempted murder – do not even have the decency to make your remorse tangible, offer me a drink or something … What do you suppose we should do to avoid handcuffing you and carting you off to jail, where you belong?' I am about to answer, but he interjects, all frowns and spittle: 'Know – in case you are beginning to have funny thoughts, strange ideas – that I have not and will never ask anyone for a bribe. You making your remorse visible, in my books, does not equate to a bribe, but to a gesture of mutual understanding, given your evident troubles with the law. In case you are tempted by the dictates of conscience to judge or frown upon my innocent request for cool drink given the scorching heat, be reminded that attempted murder is punishable, harshly and decisively.' There is a brief pause. 'So … how about that drink?'

'I have nothing to drink in the car,' I say, sheepishly.

'I imagine you have heard of a wallet, in which money is kept?'

'I have. What do you drink, or how much is your drink?'

'Use your discretion, but consider your many and varied crimes.'

'But the Traffic Management Act makes no provision for motorists buying drinks for traffic officers,' I say, in guarded irritation.

'As you please,' he says, stepping away from the vehicle to join the huddle of traffic officers who have emerged from their vehicle to flag off an elderly gentleman in a collector's Rolls-Royce. He turns his back, ignoring me entirely, and lets me stew in the blazing sun while he and his cohorts reprimand the old man for an offence I have missed. Finally, the Rolls-Royce gone, Bezuidenhout shares a joke with his fellow officers, laughs a guttural, belly roar. All this time I remain in my car, not sure of what to make of his abuse. It dawns on me how little I have spoken, how he has dominated our exchange with impunity.

'How much?' I ask him when he finally ambles over.

That tooth stabs the air, as he says, 'Two thousand six hundred rands.' There is a mind game at play … Why am I suddenly so timid, outmanoeuvred by this slob with the protruding tooth, the articulate solicitor of bribes who trades in fear? He reminds me there is a distant but distinct possibility of sodomy in jail, that three or thirteen per cent of traffic infringements could, if not properly handled, completely ruin a life. Am I prepared for that? Yes, I am, I tell him – and not only that, I am looking forward to spending the rest of my life, if I have to, tracking down his boss, for an opinion on random cool drinks expected to drop from the sky!

Bezuidenhout is suddenly conciliatory. 'I suppose,' he says, 'I can look the other way this once.'

'No!' I charge. 'I demand a fine, an arrest, anything but lectures from you!'

He chuckles, a nervous laugh: 'I was joking with you … Can't you take a joke?'

'No, I cannot. I demand to be arrested, to be held accountable for my varied sins! You get paid, don't you? I don't think you get paid in stones? Why can't you buy your own goddamn drinks?' I demand my expired licence, an unfortunate and embarrassing oversight, then flatten the accelerator to the floor, and leave a fidgety Bezuidenhout in a cloud of blue tyre smoke.

I have not always been a writer. My beginnings are humble – laughable even, often too embarrassing to share with strangers. I started my career reporting on burst water pipes, then graduated to all sorts of damage meted out by Cape Town's freak storms, a paragraph or two on page fourteen about a puppy that defied death in some clogged Kensington drain, before a stroke of luck catapulted me to occasional reports on real accidents: bikers decapitated in motorcycle crashes, gas-leak explosions in local eateries, prostitutes running riot against abusive police. I was subsequently promoted to the obituary pages, where I reported on the deaths of eminent persons of average influence, and finally to theatre reviews, which our then editor, my father, read with good humour and relish. I mistook this for a nod at my journalistic excellence, until he tamed my euphoria with sudden and cutting criticism: 'Your reviews are ambitious but confused.'

It was only two years later, having reviewed a rock concert – some amateur band called the Blazing Pistols – that Father, who read every word of the paper without fail (crossword puzzles, astrological predictions and court orders), congratulated me. 'You have some literary ghosts lurking inside of you, plus an ear for music,' he opined. 'But you got the name of the band wrong! Blaring Pistols is not the same as Blazing Pistols. That means your review, strictly speaking, doesn't count for shit.' I was stung, dispirited. I remember the embarrassment to this day, but am grateful that Father insisted I focus on and complete my literature studies.

Sixteen Doves Drive. Little Bombay is a secluded and architecturally pleasing haven frequented by introverts and retired millionaires, a laid-back address with whiffs of curries and

Indian-cum-Moroccan spices that sometimes serves as a liberating retreat loved by gorgeous single women reading *Time* magazine. It is, on unpredictable and therefore out-of-the-blue occasions, pleasing to wave, nod or flash a modest and neutral smile at such women, as absorbed as they are in all manner of things: business pages in newspapers, chuckling at private messages on cellphones, dictating firm instructions to some secretary or assistant back at the office:

'Samantha, please check availability of flights to Rio de Janeiro. Book for both me and Sizwe in Marketing, and remember to send the financials to the Board before Thursday. One more thing ... let's do something about the paint fumes in my office. I would have imagined renovations would have waited until December? You can hardly be productive while drunk on paint fumes, can you? Sorry, what was that? Yes. Aha. No, not the entire thing. Call me as soon as Beckett is out of his meeting, and cancel that conference call with the lawyers. Thanks, dear. Later then.'

Innocent eavesdropping. Nothing criminal, but an appreciation of the fact that people do still talk, and that because ears hear (curiosity, boredom, literary instincts), conversations about paint fumes and trips to Rio get absorbed.

It was three years ago, behind the not-so-attractive woman and her trip to Rio, two tables near the far end of an elevated wooden deck, below which giant goldfish cruised in lazy glides through make-believe reeds and river stones, that I first spotted Alexis, committed to a smallish bowl of pasta, skilfully stabbing and twisting her fork. She was a stranger then, strikingly beautiful in her lonesomeness. It was not her looks that attracted me, but her precise fork movements. I am, to this day, not sure if she ignored my nod or whether she mistook it for acknowledgement of something unrelated to her. It is possible that she did not see me nodding at her, my gaze friendly but cautious while at the same time following those quick-fire instructions from that Rio-bound office-renovations victim.

It was the exactness, the tempo and flow with which that pasta was eaten, without sauce accidents or resorting to urgent mouth dives over the bowl to redirect a lone pasta strand intent on spoiling immaculate table manners, that caught my attention. It was all in the chewing: just enough effort to eat, not the intrusive mashing of jaws, the lip smacking and sucking sounds that plague the uncivilised. That fork. Her slightly tilted head. The lifting motion to the delicate mouth. The opening of that mouth such that it formed an imperfect O, yet sufficient to allow the fork to deliver its noodles and mince, the O again closing at the exact moment the fork was pulled out, allowing that subtle chewing to commence – after which a glass of white wine was lifted by the very bottom of the glass stem, maybe secretly sniffed, before the minutest of sips, followed again by that wonderful waltz with the fork.

I grew thirsty watching her, felt a peculiar heat linger along my spine, hesitate along my waistline, totally ignore my loins, before speeding to the head, infecting me with throbbing temples. Those eyes of hers. It was precisely at another detail – me observing her adjust the napkin over her blouse: floral – that I learned she had a gift for movement. Nothing as crude as simple locomotion, but a natural grace, a grace unaware of its magnetic power, a power to induce thirst. This is what I, following introductions ('Alexis', 'Milton'), told her of my obsessive observance of her romance with a dish of pasta. It turned out she had been entirely unaware of me observing her every move.

'But I felt it,' she said to my utter astonishment.

'How does that happen?' I asked, puzzled and intrigued.

It was during this first interaction, too, that I learned she is a dancer, that dancers – like musicians – thrive on instincts, on the anticipation of things, on sensual awareness. It was a long conversation, prompt and captivating, during which we, upon my insistence, shared a bottle of Eben Sadie Columella. A mistake must not be made that I thus became unaware of other things happening around me. I, to prove I was not in a trance, noticed that the would-be visitor to Rio had a small scar on the left wrist, most likely a burn, that one of the waiters – the tall, bald one – walked with the slightest of limps, permanent because he was possibly born that way, that there were tomato sauce bottles missing on Tables 12, 8 and 3, and that someone, clumsy and indifferent, had dropped a lone French fry under a reed chair at Table 14, attracting a battalion of ants. I was also aware that someone had changed the ambient music, discreetly replacing the pipe music with non-intrusive piano concertos, and that someone deeper within Little Bombay was conversing in Shona.

I was, of course, also enthralled by the cooing of pigeons on some rooftop in the vicinity, and the koi that took turns zig-zagging the water feature … and then there was suddenly Alexis, the gorgeous stranger with her pasta artistry, whose stilettos placed her between 30 and 33, whose temperament suggested an introvert, whose eyes mirrored an industrious, focused mind. Her dress sense suggested a refinement, with an artistic streak lurking among her arm bracelets, her neat dreadlocks. That is how we met, Alexis and I; how we got drunk together; how I invited her to Casablanca Estates.

I looked her straight in the eyes, dreamy and reflective, and said: 'Tell me something, dear lady, Alexis – such a musical name, bestowed on such a delightful specimen – what will it take for me to seize your thoughts from this moment to eternity? Are you spiritual, philosophical, flexible or practical about access to your heart?' The questions were like lightning bolts, and though she dismissed me as cocky and unpolished, it was evident that no one had ever been so direct with her, and in her annoyance – which was shallow and not in the least convincing – succumbed to my unforeseen wooing, a charge that said: I am not like the others, and to prove this, I have laid my soul on railway tracks of chance, at the risk of murderous ego trains, trains without known schedules and reliable stopovers.

The most charming thing about Alexis is her curiosities. Months into our courting, I found her engaged in a puzzling but nevertheless intriguing experiment. She had bought four bathroom scales, which she lay lengthwise – to accommodate my height of 1.74 metres – on the wooden floors of my apartment. She asked that I lie face down across the scales. But why? 'To measure how heavy you are, more or less, five to fifteen seconds after you have ravaged me into submission, collapsed in a lump of pleasured flesh, my legs still wide open.'

I was startled. Her playful smile suggested she was skilled in the realm of the erotic. Not being a scientist, I told her, limited the quality and accuracy of my opinions, but nevertheless proceeded to point out to her that her measurements would not be accurate, given a few important variables she may not have considered, namely that though most men collapse after firing their cannons, the resultant weight onto the woman below cannot be consistent. That there were also secondary but critical factors that come into play: the beauty and fragility of the woman, the intensity or lack of participation in the deed, the quality of the bed and mattress springs – assuming such pleasures are pursued on a bed, but noting that such can be anywhere: discreet park benches, mall restrooms, the dining table, against tree trunks, in cemeteries, even aircraft ablution cages. That the hard wooden floor was also not comparable to a sixteen-year-old mattress playing host to an assortment of passionate adults. Therefore, her experiment had, more poignantly, omitted a fundamental determinant to the consistency or fluctuation of weight: the marriage between pleasure and gravity.

She smiled. 'That is why I said *more or less.*'

This made me happy; a feeling that fell like snowflakes, like confetti showered on couples at weddings, like raindrops illuminated by car headlights, fireworks exploding sky high in magnificent, temporary fiery arrangements, falling back to earth in languid, crystal, dazzling, smoky slow motion.

'Our theatre manager, a dear friend of mine, Portia,' she continued, 'who is single and not looking, who might never look, and if she does look would not look at writer types, and if she decides not to look intends on casual affairs with confident and intelligent men in uniform, affairs that will completely and totally be of her design and control, in which she reserves the right to allow and veto everything ... Well, she thinks you're sweet. Has read all your books. She wants you to speak to her lover, if you're keen. Portia complains that Marcus, her on-again-off-again lover of seven years, has clearly never *been* with a woman. And I don't mean some hurried taming of lust. I mean really *being* with a woman, being permanently marked, emptied of wants, transformed. That secret, the transformation, is not something she can explain, for men have lived and died – entire family trees across generations and continents – without the faintest hint of what it means to *be* with a woman: a spiritual, profound, elusive epiphany. Marcus, says Portia, cannot confidently say he has, even remotely, courted such a feeling. One of total surrender. That's what men look for when whoring, I suppose. Anyway … think about it.'

But I never got to speak to either Portia or Marcus. Portia died from a bee sting to the throat at Marcus' fortieth birthday lunch. Marcus was arrested the same evening for dealing in cocaine; released and rearrested a week later, then released again and was rumoured to be in hiding somewhere in Johannesburg. See? Trouble. Strange things follow me.

I think of Alexis pleasurably. Every thought of her, no matter how insignificant, throbs with sensation and longing, leaving me thirsty, and on selected occasions, with animated dreams. Looking at her, Alexis seems ageless. She has dreamy eyes, the size of baby tomatoes, perfectly proportioned features and a physique that sets her miles apart from the dreary and pitiful worlds of ugly women. In high heels she has height too, but without them she is short and bouncy. Of course, she has personality – although to say that is in itself saying very little. Which may be why some writers frown so much: at the futility of trying to sense, capture and convincingly communicate the elusive.

What isn't elusive, evident for all to see – and, I suppose, proof that Alexis has personality – is her collection of smiles, each perfected to particular causes or moments. In her smiles I detect traces of doubt, empathy, amusement, the erotic, inquisition, thought, fondness, rare confusion and distant irritation. I see displeasure, concern, despair, apprehension, disapproval. I see even her valiant recovery from weeping, her responses to pleasures of the palate in trendy restaurants, mild drunkenness from the occasional glass of red over lunch, her consciousness of both nudity and nakedness (nude suggests a certain measure of beauty and control, naked is the stuff of concentration camps), her off-key embarrassments, her vulnerability around hounds. Her vault of smiles further stores those to express other emotions – distinctly but with minute adjustments, as she responds to the sensual charges of earlobe nibbling under the cover of cinema darkness, her hypersensitivity to errant touches of the soles of her feet during intimate foot-rub rituals, specific smiles devoted to her discreet desire to be left alone, and I suppose variations of as-yet-undiscovered smiles that I might never see.

Alexis is also very much a creature of sound. When it comes to her auditory worlds, it would be reasonably accurate to say that she thrives within low-decibel realms where everything seems trimmed of sound. Except for the momentary rustle of bed sheets every three hours or so, she is a soundless sleeper. Her undisclosed power over sound is one of silence. Apart from accidental clatters (a coffee mug shattering on the tiles, a door blown shut, the alarm of her Mini Cooper daydreaming), I have never, for instance, once heard Alexis' urine land on the water in the toilet bowl, or her teaspoon scrapping a teacup as she stirs, or ecstatic pleasure chants during our civilised mating. Instead of some noisy declaration, as if a call for signatures for a revolutionary public petition, there is a smile, a twitchy quarter-smile accompanied by a momentary hint of a frown, one that matures into a half-smile, and then seamlessly into a seven-second grin, an almost inaudible confession of 'I love you'.

When it comes to smell Alexis has limitations. A chronic case of sinusitis and a shopping list of allergies have obscured any observations of her as a creature of smell. The world's smells are lost to her, and yet she still takes three showers a day, offering whiffs of floral scents by way of pricy perfumes, combinations that make me want to kiss the nape of her neck, taste Mediterranean plant life, absorb the traces of whatever oils are used in such fragrances.

It was clear, though, that Alexis' sinus treatment was working and that she began to smell again: fruit, meals, the tongue-molesting scones she baked; the way she would say, '*O nkga bose motho waka. Batamela ke go sware ka ditsebe.*' – You smell nice, my love. Come closer – let me hold you by the ears.

Her sensual sensibilities shall, in the interests of decency, remain privileged information, except for a minor detail, which I believe to be universal to women and not necessarily particular to Alexis: she adores being touched, but not necessarily in the erotic sense. Touch in its widest definition and implication: hugs, hand holding, foot massages, my lips colliding with her inspirational ears when I lean over and confess grave and naughty intentions in conspiratorial whispers.

Being an artist at heart, of the subtle but intense kind, Alexis seems to have been born with a gracious maturity. At twenty-six, she exudes a quiet charm often mistaken for confidence, but is in fact a deep sense of knowing, of trusting, moving in concert with life and its imperfections.

Those varied smiles of hers. Her Michelangelo-carved back, with hints and curvatures that confirm flawless balance. Skin without the slightest blot. Yet she has one disconcerting flaw: Alexis is hopelessly forgetful. Our conversations, our plans, our lives, our very existence are premised on constant reminders, serious contemplations quadruple checked and adjusted to the immediacy and depth of what she remembers. How my heart leaps when she recalls particular episodes with detective clarity and detail. When in that mode of grand recollections, her mind remembers the minutiae: venues, seat numbers, temperature readings, significant breaking news, names of manufacturers of dining utensils used in specific restaurants, that the traffic light (red, the danger one) a block away from where we sat, indulging on honey and nuts in Greek yoghurt, had blown a fuse. When life is a blur, when she is in her forgetful mode, I either start our conversations with 'Remember ...' or 'Do you recall ...' or 'Actually ...'. It is pleasurable in the extreme when she remembers things, reorders and interprets them with remarkable precision.

As a dancer, her body is always hinting at movement, timing, all her gliding across the apartment, her pauses, holds, sudden bursts of energy, all completed with an elaborate theatrical bow. She was lucky, mentored by former Alvin Ailey veterans, New

Yorkers, and combined with her natural instinct for movement, turned into a commanding dancer, an accomplished performer. I attend all her shows, matinées included. I watch all her rehearsal tapes, study all her stills, and perch myself unanimously in full-capacity theatres, surrendering to her fluid movements, episodes that make the depths of my ears itch, my mouth twitch, my senses ache. I, weeks in advance, insist on selecting her curtain-call flowers, a combination of roses and tulips, to be presented to her amid thunderous applause during those fifteen-minute standing ovations. It is at such moments that I remain seated, cover my face with a scarf or my Ray-Bans, succumb to a brief but pleasurable sob, overwhelmed by the beauty and intensity of it all. I am defenceless against art. Everything I have read, from multiple sources (not excluding expert commentary), suggests that dance is both a *memory* and *movement* art, a craft built on timing and anticipation, and above all spatial awareness. How my forgetful Alexis pulls it off amazes me – how she never misses a single step, how effortless she makes everything seem. This is, in part, what I mean when I say: I think of her pleasurably.

I fall asleep thinking about her, dream a strange dream – long, old, in black-and-white, documentary-type pictures, a dream in which I become someone else entirely.

Omaha Beach

That was not supposed to happen. What I had been told, assured of, convinced myself would happen, did not. It all went catastrophically wrong. It is predictable and to be expected that I sleep badly, that I often wake drenched in sweat, my voice hoarse from screaming, that I lie awake listening to crickets and my knotted bowels squirm, to the grinding of what is left of my clenched teeth. My hearing is no longer dependable, my sight clouded by doubt and illusion, my mobility a source of angst and despair. My spirit is not irredeemably dampened, though: I chuckle once in a while, am grateful for restful sleep that is both rare and priceless, wink at the odd stranger whose eyebrows tickle my fancy. I had hoped that I would die within six months of George Bush Senior leaving office, even though I am in relatively good health for my age and despite the cranking and wheezing of a spent body yearning for its grave.

See that picture? Multitudes of strong and not-so-strong young men with hazy life plans and pimples drafted into

Roosevelt's army, shepherded like sheep from states all around our Union – Indianapolis, Washington, Iowa, Mississippi, Kentucky, and others – to bomb, take over and die for towns and bridges whose names we couldn't properly pronounce.

See that one? No, not the one with a puppy. That's a painting, a very bad attempt at animal art. I mean the small, faded picture at my bedside. The handsome guy with an unlit smoke in his mouth, clutching a rifle, bare breasted, grinning at the camera? That's me. I don't remember any of the fools in the picture with me, but I sure remember Private Washington. He saved my life. The smoke you see in the background, and those faded lines with water damage, those are Bastogne ruins in flames, moments after we wiped out an entire German infantry unit. I was given a medal for it – and am, to this day, considered a national treasure of sorts, highly decorated, respected, have private lunch with the president kinda thing. As tank gunners go, I was – and perhaps still am – the best in the business. A hundred German Tigers to two American tanks lost. Some record. There was and still is talk in Washington and elsewhere that my record remains one of the most admirable achievements in the dying moments of the war. Bear in mind that I was not even a trained gunner, but a sniper.

I am a self-styled military historian of sorts. Our gunships were supposed to gallantly charge on the Pacific, our bomber squadrons roaring above us in tight formation, hearts thumping and guns at the ready. Our troops were supposed to open their shoots and bloom the morning sky as we descended on Omaha Beach. We were supposed to incinerate an inferior enemy, one that was ill equipped, with low morale, little-experienced dregs of the German army. Instead, we were slaughtered. Thousands of our boys and those from the Allied forces never made it to the beach. Those German snipers and machine gunners picked us off like flies, bloodying the waters, littering the shoreline with corpses. No one expected the place to be so well fortified, that countless fingers rested on triggers, waiting for us to show face. Encircled by barbed wire, decapitated and half-burned bodies, surrounded by the drowning wounded, the rattle of machine-gun fire, flying debris and torched vehicles, the wheezing of bullets, silent morning mist and the indifferent humming of a restless sea, amid courage and cowardice and the smell of death, I somehow survived. Private Washington was not that lucky. He was mummifying my head with bandage, a wound inflicted by some unknown projectile of metallic form, when a sniper's bullet blew his face to smithereens, leaving an almost headless corpse twitching on the beach sand. It was the strangest thing, seeing and smelling and touching remnants of death at such a scale. And the bullets and mortars kept coming. And coming. And ripping through flesh. And helmets. And bones. They were quite something, those Normandy landings. But we managed somehow – with reinforcements and more corpses – to walk into German bullets, secure Omaha, an inch, a corpse at a time. Everything was a haze, distant and nerve-wracking, until I found myself, a week later, en route to the frontlines.

There is a sensual beauty, an artistry, a kind of detached satisfaction in killing somebody in the snow. All that bleeding, red against white, the helpless twitching, the hot breath that escapes the mortally wounded carcass as victims groan in prayer, pain and despair. A single clap of the rifle and the bullet speeds past snow-draped foliage, determined in its deathly obligations, among falling snowflakes, tearing through the icy invisible wind to a target a thousand yards away.

That was, as winters go, perhaps the coldest, with traces of all sorts of mock warmth that console an indifferent heart. I had not felt my feet for sixteen days straight, and feared frostbite, amputations that would befall my lovely toes if the snow triumphed. Body count? One hundred and twenty. Four Germans were saved by winds interfering with my rounds, or me unexpectedly running out of ammunition. The worst thing about that war was, as with other wars I suppose, not being shipped to face the tanks, not the paralysing cold, not belly-gnawing bouts of hunger and thirst and pounding headaches that can immobilise even the most enraged and suicidal of soldiers, not missing Elisabeth's plump thighs, between which Massachusetts mornings found me smiling and content. The worst was not all the seasickness and throwing up, not the fighter-bombers that stalked us from above or the submarines with their deadly stealth below. It was not Roosevelt in his wheelchair signing all sorts of orders that committed infantryman upon infantryman to a gory death. Not the booby traps and enemy tricks that kept us on our toes. Not dreaming colourful dreams against tree trunks only to wake to the barrage of cannon fire. Not dragging wounded comrades blown to shreds by German mortars or machine guns, nor the horror of bloody intestines spilling out onto the innocent snow. It was not being captured, lined up and executed by impromptu German firing squads, to say nothing of being mistakenly left for dead. It was not the searing stories of torture and abuse at the hands of enemy intelligence, hell, not even missing Elisabeth's girly laughter. It wasn't humming Christmas carols in the company of mangled corpses – some with looks of surprise or rage on their faces, not the boots and water bottles and knives we took from the dead on our march to Berlin. It was not missing my dear friend Eddie, saved from war duties by polio and bad eyesight, or that abandoned novel of mine, which Peter Bellow at Three Nations Press said showed much promise. It was not stolen merry-go-round conversations with Matilda, whom I should and could have married were it not for our fathers being mortal enemies, nothing to do with salt shortages and food rations suffered by good-hearted Americans because of and in spite of the war. No, it was that anxiety, that palpable tension, that cold shadow: when and how death was likely to come.

We were commanded by Major E Summers, who farted freely and chewed tobacco, who was brutal but not without being somewhat kind, who famously carried the wounded Private Marcus Smith a mile and a half in deep snow, who bled on his boot heels and left a winding trail of blood – a dead giveaway to observing enemy snipers. Marcus died of asphyxiation from being carried upside down.

I, as we ploughed through the exhausting snow, wondered how my death would come, whether it would be sudden and painless, if it would mean anything at all, how it would be recorded. It became very dangerous to even empty one's bladder or bowels without the ever-present possibility of a German sniper shooting your testicles off. So we stood guard over fellow infantrymen who fancied a peaceful shit, acting as their eyes and ears as it were, half joking yet dead serious in warning: 'Dump quick, dammit, you want to get us shot?' That is how Ryan Somerset from Maine perished, how Gilbert Stones and John Woodpeck – Illinois boys, distant cousins – watched in horror as sniper bullets carved a smoky path right under Private Somerset's bare buttocks, how his spine was shredded by machine-gun fire right in front of their eyes. We marched, drove, with little food or sleep, and ended up facing even more bullets.

We held Bastogne at great cost. I saw an SS man aim a mortar at me. In fact, I saw him load it, maintain eye contact, take aim. I could, from my elevated position on the second floor of a house in ruins, peeping through a half-collapsed wall decorated with bullet holes, make out at least three German Tigers scouting for victims, their commanders, binoculars at the ready, gallantly surveying the battlefield with chilling purpose and calm. I was sleep deprived and irritable, and should have, when he raised the gun to his shoulder, taken cover, scuttled out of the way. But I couldn't. I still think about my reason for daring that mortar that day, but cannot fathom what it could have been. I wasn't wounded, was reasonably mobile, sleepy but alert and, best of all, had at least two full minutes with which to aim my rifle and blow that cocky bastard to hell. It wasn't suicidal thoughts, not daring God, it wasn't even laziness. As the mortar left his gun, tearing through the ruins with that unmistakeable whistle, like burned pineapple in flight, three interesting developments unfolded: I lost control of my bladder; I was suddenly thirstier than I had ever been in all of my life; I mouthed Psalm 23 without urgency or hope. There was a deafening pop, then everything was smoky and silent, distant. So violent and close was the explosion that for five minutes the war ended, the world ceased to exist.

I was flung through a concrete wall, and landed face down in a cloud of dust and flying debris. The earth rotated beneath me, the thirst slowed my breathing, and for a moment I could not feel my legs. 'Shoot me,' I choked as someone gripped my collar and dragged me to safety, dodging bullets and shells, until I was positioned against a wall. I tasted blood. My left ear bled.

It was not supposed to happen that way, but heavy shelling and me presumably buried under rubble meant that my platoon pulled back without me. So instead of a comrade, I opened my eyes to find a tall German commandant staring at me with guarded disdain, a sense of curiosity and deadly charm. He lit a cigarette, then another.

'You speak German?' came a question, his hand extending me a lit cigarette.

I had, until that point, never smoked in my life. But it was not every day, I thought, that an enemy, armed to the teeth, offered you a cigarette. It must have been in the way I held it, how my hand trembled, the coughing and choking that followed that gave me away. He squatted in front of me, so close I could see his chipped tooth, the veins in his green eyes. He had a discreet smile, strong facial features that suggested authority and insolence. Five other men, rifles drawn, made their way through the ruins, and rooted themselves a few paces behind their commander. Light streaks from bullet holes in the crumbling wall suggested some elusive beauty, of light embracing dust and cigarette smoke, illuminating shadows with effortless indifference. The commander gently reached out, pulled the cigarette from my mouth, quashed it under his muddy boots.

I had a new appreciation for the quality of German bones, German veins, German uniforms; was in complete awe of how methodical and composed some men could be, even with bullets flying all around us.

'I see you don't smoke. That is okay. I must commend your manners, though. You simply accepted the cigarette without questions or judgement, and that, my friend, is very impressive. Most men get shot not because they are unlucky, or unskilled, or hasty or untrained; they die because they have no manners. Manners. You have displayed admirable virtue, exemplary conduct that touches me deeply – and for that reason,' he said half-turning, addressing his men, 'you have impunity against death. For as long as I am alive, no one is to shoot this man. No one.' But that did not mean, he added, that I would escape the suffering to be expected during a time of war, including some disturbing transgressions regarding the treatment of POWs; it only meant that such tortures, known and hidden, were to never result in me dying. He snapped his finger, and someone threw a German army uniform from the rafters, crisp and new, wrapped in brown paper.

'Shoe size?'

'Nine.'

He looked around at his men, resting his gaze on the young one bleeding from the elbow onto the concrete floor, and requested he surrender his boots. 'Those look to me to be size nines.' He gently, leisurely pulled out his pistol, aimed at the bleeding and now bootless soldier, and shot him twice in the chest. None of the men stirred. Not a single wince.

He shook my hand, said: 'Commandant Althaus.'

'Gomez,' I nodded. 'Giovanni Gomez.'

He smiled, nodded in turn.

His men had rounded up what remained of my platoon, all twelve of us, for what he called *Die Realität des Krieges* – the Realities of War. I thought that meant taking us as POWs, since we made no qualms about surrendering, our faces pitiful and defeated. He lined us up, all facing the wall, among the ruins, all twelve of us, sons of our mothers and fathers and, with the calmest resolve, asked our names, ranks, hobbies, marital status, whether we had any offspring. Then he personally shot eleven, in strict alphabetical order, confiscated their cigarettes and motioned that I start walking alongside his motorcycle.

My captor, Commandant Althaus, was – according to him – of Austrian leanings, a tall man with dimples and a twinkle in his eyes. His gopher posture, upright and alert, complimented his good looks and wry humour, so that just being around him lent a sense of occasion. He had big feet, was ageing gracefully, and had certainly benefited from the precisions of military life (walk, eye contact, admirable command of his senses) and I suspected that he, when he let his guard down, could make a very impressive father-in-law indeed. Ashy elbows and big ears should hardly be criteria when assessing a man's worth, I know, but I assume he was also a skilled and trusted commander. And yet I knew nothing more about my captor, except that he was German.

My eardrum sore and occasionally bleeding, my balance shattered, and my walk wobbly, I – dressed in the SS uniform of a man twice my size, and boots that were inordinately large for a size nine – marched through the fumes of Commandant

Althaus' motorcycle. He, very sternly but politely, instructed me to keep marching alongside, even with the seat of his military sidecar vacant. He ensured, though, that my march was not without rewards. When we approached a gathering of resting German infantry, he offered me water, a hunk of canned meat that tasted like rubber, and after a long and I suppose enjoyable yawn, invited me to take the seat in the sidecar.

I was, eight days later, my oversized SS uniform almost frozen from the snow, riding alongside him in the sidecar when Althaus turned to me.

'The man whose boots you have the pleasure of inheriting was a notorious deserter. We can't have that in the German army – these part-time soldiers. It is not good for morale, for all the dedicated, respectable and gallant Germans risking their lives for the Fatherland. They too want to help themselves to restful sleep, a night with a French virgin, hot baths earned from badmouthing the Führer.'

I was, as I sat alongside him, offered water. Bread. The occasional sausage. Snippets of German history. It was only twenty miles later that Commandant Althaus burst out laughing and asked if I thought I was in any danger, and thus put me at ease. He again commended my good manners, my soldierly discipline. He watched me as we rode, passed through the remnants of shelled neighbourhoods, the smell of war ever present. As Bastogne became a distant memory, we arrived in a little town, unknown and mercilessly bombed. I observed in passing: that used to be a church, that a windmill, that fluffy stench perhaps a dog, that over there a bridge, and these ruins once a town pulsing with human dreams and dead potential.

At Leipzig we boarded a truck, a train in Berlin, before a motorcade ride to Rastenburg, East Prussia, to what I came to know as the *Wolfschanze* – the Wolf's Lair – a place of tall trees and eerie tranquillity. I was dozing in the car, the rumble of its engine threatening to plunge me into deep sleep. Commandant Althaus handed me over to two stern officers, who, despite Althaus' strict instructions that I not be ill-treated, grabbed my collar and frogmarched me past a series of buildings, guarded checkpoints and down a staircase that seemed to never end.

I am possibly the only American infantryman to have stood within paces of the Führer without being shot. He was not the fanatical, saliva-spewing, impassioned orator of Goebbels' film footage. Not the concrete-faced, otherworldly misfit with piercing eyes, or the map-pointing Napoleon in search of a vast empire and immortality. He was quite ordinary, of no prominent physical presence, in a state of permanent discomfort – not the most remarkable of human specimens. It was almost impossible for me to believe that he was in fact *him*, dressed in an ill-fitting suit and a civilian hat, walking with a stick, mornings and afternoons, with an assortment of confidants, including Blondi, the German Shepherd. Even during seemingly engaged convers-ations, with military men and other confidants craning their necks to hear every word, he remained detached from the real world. Aloof. Unsure. And yet there remained a strange charisma to his gestures, how he saluted the multitude of kindred spirits who crossed his path, whispered instructions to aides, who nodded their total reverence at even the smallest of his gestures.

I later learned that the man was very nearly a corpse, because someone – someone trusted – had attempted to blow him to smithereens with a suitcase bomb just weeks earlier. I had it on good authority that there were impromptu executions of real and suspected conspirators. There were, apparently, voluntary and forced confessions to the failed assassination attempt, the main cause of which was disarmingly simple: some Germans were tired of the war, tired of bombing raids, their homes and churches and cities and country reduced to ruins. It confirmed, at least to me, that there were a few – maybe many, for there was no way of telling – who resisted the Führer and his scheming, his Napoleonic jitters. And yet, and yet, in his unsure sureness, summers and winters were filled with planning and plotting, filled with maps and bombs and threats, riddled with spies, declarations, ultimatums and explosions intent on subjugation. I wondered what he thought about when he was not banging a fist on a table, pointing on maps, barking shrill-voiced commands to sceptical but committed commandants. Did he whisper in Eva's ear? Was he a fondler, a wet kisser, did he kiss with his eyes closed? Were his private passions halted by phone calls or deciphered Morse code horrors from the Atlantic, from Stalingrad, from Omaha Beach? Did he see himself as a fanatic, or as simply passionate, patriotic? What were all those walks in the woods about, those moments of reflection – balming a burdened conscience, or attempts to rein in that increasingly shaky hand of his? What did he think about when naked under shower nozzles? Did he pinch his pouching belly fat, inspect contours of his buttocks, wish an awkward belly button away?

How did such a paranoid man – the same man who drove food tasters to the brink of insanity, skirmishes with fate, tasting his food to ensure it had not been poisoned – allow that Doctor Morell to inject him with things? I saw the food tasters, haggard and of fragile posture, burdened, tasting his dishes, throwing the dice, gambling with their very lives in an effort to safeguard the Führer. What went through their minds, the poor, wretched things, with all their knowing of the unknown, of which dish would be poisoned with which stomach-corroding agents, which droplets would make them foam at the mouth and suffer fits? What did they think of food: of beans, soup, tea? Was it for them – despite its obvious dangers, of suspect nutrition – a liveable terror that one simply got used to, just as some people learn to work in mortuaries, among corpses? What did they think of their gambling with death, being its gatekeepers? Was it just a matter of being in a perpetual state of acting sacrificial lambs? How was it that some lives could be rendered so worthless, like chaff or mud, less than straw, which still retains at least some value as animal feed?

Of course the *Wolfschanze* had impressive routines, a certain aura of authority and secrecy, but it lacked a very basic ingredient that would have made it humane: affection. All those uniformed men, food tasters, dogs and all, clung to an idea of a leader who was in truth not only elusive (I saw him only twice, both times quite by accident) but a recluse. There was a coldness about the man, even when he smiled – a smile, I believe, he thought warm and welcoming. And yet, apart from habits learned from military regimentation (posture, salutes, counted footsteps from marching), I witnessed within a three-minute time window a peculiar warmth, an affability, even childish abandon when he played with the dogs, when Eva smiled and waved at him from the car, surrounded by doyens of the Third Reich.

I was, as Commandant Althaus promised, never ill-treated – something that unnerved me to the very core. I was afforded a haircut every eighth day, a clean SS uniform, and access to a radio that spewed what was certainly not German, probably Slovac, possibly Hungarian. I was put up in an underground room tastefully furnished, afforded a comfortable bed with crisp white sheets. The shower there remains one of the warmest and most generous liaisons I have had with water, its thunderous nozzles whipping the body with steamy and calming jets. I had no reading material, limited human contact, and grey walls against which to bounce my thoughts – back and forth, sideways, up and down, all the way up, beyond the stratosphere, back down to earth and sunken depths as deep as oceans – as to why I had not been lined up against the wall and shot. Why had I been spared, when the rest of my platoon were summarily executed? How was it possible that I was afforded creature comforts? Were others being shot, hanged, starved? How many? For what crimes? Could their crimes be pardoned, reconsidered, overlooked? What was I doing, dressed like that, mocked, in German military regalia? Was I being fattened for the kill, with all those sausages and beans and good bread?

Why was Marie Amsel assigned to me? Was she my slave, forced to attend to my every whim, or was I being trapped, secretly observed, should I make a confession of some kind? Or were they laughing into their pillows at my utter paralysis, my fear and cowardice, at Marie who dwells too long bending over, pouring tea, her breasts pulsing in concealed revelations, her hips the very essence of form, that neck adorned with a silver chain that ends in a crucifix, a tiny Jesus that now and again threatens to take a swim in my teacup? Those calves of hers, shapely without being athletic, those feminine hands free of a wedding band, the smile that quivered in hesitation and intensity. Was it even possible to consider love, let alone fall in it? What did she know, Marie, that made her so nervous, so edgy? How grave were secrets that made her lose colour and pallor, lapse into momentary sighs? What heavy burdens, other than the servitude without conversation, weighed her down? What rewards, what perks did servitude to prisoners of war attract? What of the daring middle-of-the-night knocks at my door, the out-of-place permission to soak in my bathtub so deep it could accommodate Churchill, Stalin and Roosevelt in one merry bath? What were those thrice-a-week soaks in the bath, sometimes at three in the morning, without a word of explanation? Was she bait to test the very limits of my manners? Would laying a hand on her enrage Commandant Althaus so that he would line me up against a wall and execute me? What if casting a blind eye, being indifferent, was itself contrary to expectations? What if Marie was the prize for my so-called good manners?

What was obvious was that Althaus wielded considerable power, that he need only snap his fingers, speak in barely audible monotone, for all sorts of things to start happening, for people to start scampering about in response. For all my curiosities, my loins rusted from fear and no use, I convinced myself that I would walk the fine line between good manners and composure, between caution and optimism. I would not touch Marie unless explicitly so instructed by Commandant Althaus. Her fiery rump would remain her own, untouched, and her earlobes free of nibbling intrusions; her thoughts, her dreams, her passions left alone until such time that it became clear what those night bath provocations were meant to trigger or achieve.

As voluptuousness goes, Marie was nothing short of those fleshy posers in Renaissance paintings, only trimmed and more lifelike – a living, breathing human with nipples the colour and texture of strawberries. Whatever her obligations to me, it was clear that Marie had abundant freedoms, and though evidently monitored, she had minute time windows during which she could be herself, relax in a steaming bath, maybe even forget there was a war going on. Were there other Maries, spread across Berlin, Leipzig, Monowitz, in service of what prisoners?

She whispered, her eyes red from tears and a lack of sleep, that something significant was about to happen, though she was unsure what that was. The uniformed men knew, she suspected, but she couldn't be sure what it was that they knew, because no one was saying anything to anybody. They all shuffled papers, she said. Typed papers. Stamped papers. Papers concealed in manilla envelopes. Lists in giant ledgers. Handwritten notes. Construction plans. Airplane and tank sketches. Food rations. Maps of London and France and Poland and Russia and America. Papers recording concrete tonnage, train routes, assets seized. Papers recording names – prisoners and their numbers – and professions that would be obsolete.

57837 22   Zimmerman, Bettina: Doctor

57837 23   Mencher, Antoni: Poet

57837 24   Krakowski, Mateusz: Architect

57837 25   Cohen, Moses: Rabbi

57837 26   Markovic, Vladimir: Solicitor

57837 27   Pasternak, Franciszek: Diamond Polisher

57837 28   Stolarz, Albinka: Mathematician

57837 29   Bozeman, Maria: Athlete

57837 30   Goldhirsch, Adamina: Midwife

57837 31   Allen, Aaron: Tailor

There were over seventeen million others: dentists, bricklayers, butchers, other life vocations. But she knew something worth knowing, that much was clear – something that ate at her, infected her with strange fevers, deprived her of sleep. What was it that tortured her so? The documents, in part. She confessed that much, sliding into the bath, her lips painted red, slightly parted, revealing two front teeth the size of sunflower seeds. She lathered and squirmed, the soap trapped between her legs, one leg under water, the other on display, igniting all sorts of possibilities, confusions. What was Marie, pretty and perceptive, doing in the bathtub of a prisoner of war at five minutes after midnight, uninvited? Were the Führer and his confidants too busy waging a war, focused on downing planes and sinking ships and blowing up skulls, to care about Marie and her midnight baths? Or were there too many Maries scrubbing their bodies of mysterious impurities for Himmler and Eichmann to care?

How were one, ten, a million midnight baths going to stop a war? Who, of the many men in stiff and pressed uniforms, the mini emperors and minions of the *Wolfschanze*, sanctioned Marie's nocturnal liberties in my bathtub? And what of her tears, those sighs and snorting, her mumbling in the bath? It was as if oceans raged inside her, as if she was heating and cooling to my indifference, my inaction. It must be that she sensed something inside me, that though I turned my back, ignored her eager but guarded gaze, her muted sobs, there was in my depths a flicker of light, a formless silence that, even amid the drone of bombers and whistle of bullets, marked me as not cut out for taking lives. She must have felt it; it must have drawn her in, assured her that not all was lost, that there was, even with whatever burdens crippled her youth, at least one human who would, if he lives, with time, thaw a hardened heart, return her gaze.

I found it daunting that I was, vast as Germany was, confined to an underground bunker and fattened for unknown eventualities. My thoughts were a dead end, worsened by the fact that *Wolfschanze* was itself a dead end, not intended for normal living, a burrow behind the walls of which fingers pointed at maps, at routes, at bridges and military installations, at hills for the taking, in minuscule and grand attempts at swaying the outcome of the war.

Prisoners are directed, their movements and thoughts curtailed, ownership of their very bodies put into question. What happened to me should never have happened: a doctor visiting me every third day, tending to my shattered eardrum, with minimal questions and injections. A dose of morphine had kept me going for days immediately after the blast and I still find it strange that one ear has to capture and decipher the world's sounds. Footsteps. Gunshots. Sirens. Momentary gusts of wind blowing dust and leaf litter into the air. The distant drone of lorry engines. I should have been shot, not nursed. The SS uniform would have made me an easy target for my own infantry; the Germans would have shot me because I was an American who would not hesitate to shoot them on sight, and the Americans because my uniform declared me an enemy of our Founding Fathers. I mouthed the words again, under my breath: 'We hold these truths to be self-evident that all men are created equal ...'

I woke one morning to find in the room a row of boots of varied sizes: sixes, sevens, all the way to fourteens. Muddy boots. Dusty boots. Stained boots. Ashy boots. Wet boots. Boots caked with dog shit, bloody boots, boots with grass blades and those with cigarette butts trampled into their rubber soles. Marie reported that I had been tasked with polishing them, that she would return with a wheelbarrow, and in four trips, ship the shiny boots to whence they had come. Was Goebbels' among them, Hess' perhaps, or did they belong to unimportant functionaries, unimaginative enforcers, perhaps to deceased soldiers from the frontlines, or shod new converts and hardened fighters? Or were they simply boots, without owners, of no particular importance, boots that could just as well have been sandals? I could have never perceived, imagined that I would find myself forty miles east of Berlin, polishing boots while getting fat on good food and sausages. The man who looked back at me when I peered into the bathroom mirror, plump-faced with rosy cheeks, was not consistent with my otherwise chiselled features and dashing looks. I worried that I was on my way to becoming a slob, all those hours of seldom-interrupted sleep, the increasing hope that I would perhaps not be executed after all, and the overwhelming benevolence of the Reich in puzzling me with Marie, the nude midnight bather in the prime of her life, and all things sensual.

Something dramatic and unsettling happened. Marie must have been instructed to withhold her services, to bathe elsewhere, for she, without warning, stopped coming. Her cleaning and boot shipments became erratic, unpredictable, and not without tears. Whatever it was, I wished she could share her burdens, entrust her secrets to me, allow me to ask questions that had been burning me, ponderings about my own fate. But Marie's silence, her industriousness, her increasingly haggard posture, her foot shuffling, the blackening bags below her eyes and pale complexion pointed to something beyond language; that is, that even if she could share in intimate detail her discomforts, it seemed to me that such an act would worsen her condition, push her to the very edge, engender rupture.

She was not, by the sound of things, deeply conversant in English, for all her conversations were a mixture of German, English, hand gestures – but there was more to it than just her faltering communications. The tension that held her body taut and rigid suggested that she was not in command of or in agreement with the duties assigned to or imposed on her.

Someone important must have given her an ultimatum, and if not that, ensured that she was aware that there was no room for rebellion, that her opinions did not matter, that she was no different from a lamppost from which street lights hung without the pole having a say. And there were the notes too. Someone overruled her, left notes in neat cursive under my heavy oak door – instructions really; sometimes courtesy information, seldom compliments: a fire drill, changes in menu, electricity cuts due to routine maintenance.

You have to understand, though, that Marie Amsel never once behaved in any overt manner that would logically, philosophically, arguably or imaginatively lead to her being even remotely being thought of as a seductress. She was, even in her nudity during those midnight baths, head slightly bowed, eternally discreet, self-conscious, modest. There was nothing in what she did – implied or actual – that could result in her being accused of even the slightest lewdness. The reason she did what she did was obvious to the eye and the heart: hers was a burdened soul finding solace, relief, even companionship in bath water. That was not illegal, neither was it provocative, for the tragic reason that the war had quite simply blunted my instincts: I laughed without joy, hollow laughs, thought without precision, to say nothing of what a naked woman in her prime, breasts aflame with good health and admirable design, was supposed to do to a man and his carnal preoccupations.

It goes without saying that a nude woman, as form, a tangible being, living, breathing, with wants and secrets, is among the most perplexing and exhilarating experiences in the whole universe – so it was very tragic that such allure, such power, such magnetism were lost on me, without effect, redundant even. How was that possible that such a primal urge, abundant with charms and obsessions, could face ruin, lose value, be without consequence? Was the war that overpowering, that denting, that ruinous that it reordered the universe? If it was ruinous, or at least corrosive – meaning that it could be stopped, for corrosion is often a slow decline – what was I expected to do or say in order to restore balance, the natural order of things? Was it too easy a scapegoat to blame the war, or was the paralysis something more profound, a realisation of the helplessness of mortality, for instance? Or do women have their own eyes, other eyes, with which to look at and admire men? Is it a question of physique, I wondered, that men were supposed to look like Michelangelo's *David*, with near-perfect proportions? Or was the recognition of that beauty in men more an instinctive urge, that regardless of a pot belly or poor dental hygiene, could still render a man a man, masculine, desirable even? Were questions of height and wealth and humour irrelevant to some women, mastery of the trumpet and heart-melting poetry redundant, if a man didn't smell or snore like a man? Were these calculations swirling around in Marie's mind? Was I under covert assessment, to ascertain whether I was worthy enough to be trusted with her nudity? Or was her nakedness an imposition, a dictatorial gesture, her fleeting glances soaking up my shortcomings, my meagre value, my lack of mystery, the presence of which would have propelled her into my arms and, tearful and impassioned, led her to exclaim without shame or reservation: I want you, need you.

And yet I was aware that particular kinds of men, by virtue of who they are (violent brutes, elopers, men of the cloth, sons of famous fathers, jealous lovers), demand a certain tact from women – a thought-through approach on how to, for instance, tell a violent man that she is considering divorce, or a respected priest that bliss awaited if he could momentarily abandon the yokes of the spirit and embrace the carelessness of the flesh. At twenty-two, one knows little or nothing about women. The little that is known, or thought to be known, has to do with a state of disbelief and euphoric celebration – often misplaced – at some woman or other having allowed the celebrant into her life, her bed, her depths. Because decent women are so choosy as to whom they allow into their lives, it is nothing short of a small and at times profound miracle when she decides – not without pondering and reflection – to avail her soul for all sorts of triumphs and disappointments with men.

Our age judged errant hearts harshly, so much so that one felt guilty to love, even if torrent longing, urges of all kinds were endured until vows were exchanged in front of a beaming but suspicious priest. Family came, friends and masquerading enemies, to witness and envy a wedding that was, in countless instances, license to copulate without guilt, with permission given – though without proof – by God himself. The world was much slower in the 1940s, of course, full of all sorts of prohibitions, cautions, condemnations: how you looked at girls, the nature and detail of secrets you kept, whether you were related to fascists, the sacredness with which you treated entire family trees, bloodlines.

Even during the war, with Europe in flames, the Pacific swallowing ship after ship, the skies swarming with airborne death, I felt there was something very light, unburdened, carefree about me, that I was not one to be tied to things: church choirs, family traditions, football clubs, music ensembles or anything of the sort. I was and remained a lonesome soul, at my calmest and most lucid when left alone to think and doze and live according to my sensibilities – which at times included all-day chess games with myself. How I relished those games, getting to know myself; how I thought, how I deceived, my hesitations and gloating table banging when the Queen fell, when I, with three silly and absent-minded moves, cornered myself, lost and won to and against myself, so intensely that one day I woke up with hair in my pubis, never having touched a girl, but with a mind that could recite Wordsworth and the Declaration of Independence in a perfect murmur.

I was an average student, never convinced that algebra and geometry were important if I never intended building bridges or was interested in at what temperature steel would melt. I yawned a lot in class, and an aversion to hard work meant that I was never very good with my hands, a trait often mistaken for laziness. I despised routine, so baths, scheduled meals, news time on the radio, bedtime always sparked mini revolutions in me, revolutions I could never voice or act out because my father had the temper of a psychopath – a psychopath I had been killing and avenging myself against ever since I had been drafted. Every German, Pole, Russian I shot was in my mind a version of my father, shot in the many ways I fantasised about murdering him: for hitting Mother and me, drinking too much, twice vomiting at the dinner table. He told weak, transparent lies, disrespectful untruths cobbled together at the last minute, with no foresight as to how they would sound. He was cynical and religious, a strange cocktail of a being that gave him an at once benevolent and sarcastic smile. Whisky cooked his liver to the Grand Cemetery. I never attended his burial, and remain unsure whether I have lived – or will live – to regret this omission.

But, given my predicament, I was in no state to reflect on such calculations. I suspected there was very little I could do or wish for without facing a much more sobering reality: how I perceived or related to Marie depended on whether I lived or died, which was strange because I did not fear death as a concept, but rather dreaded how I would meet my demise, the extent of my as-yet-unknown suffering. One cannot compare being lined up against a wall and shot to being starved to death, for instance, one omitted meal at a time. Or being flogged and left for dead only to regain consciousness at midnight, alone, still tied to the flogging pole, or blindfolded and hanged without forewarning, or worked like a mule to the very last gasp in mindless and back-breaking work. Whichever the combination, it depended on whether or not I was kept alive.

My being holed up in a bunker did have its unintended pleasures, though: the pleasure to, for instance, see the sky, watch as a breeze robbed trees of their leaves, the privilege to cast eyes far and wide, wonder what of importance lay yonder, far into the woods. There were moments – I recall three afternoons – when I was allowed, coaxed, invited to polish my daily delivery of boots on a veranda overlooking a stable, a stable without horses. The steel chair chilled my bottom, never seemed to warm up, until I had polished all ten pairs with passion and a detached sense of reverence. These were, I suspected, boots of eminent Germans, too busy or respected to polish their own boots.

Save for a meagre collection of decorative plants, the *Wolfschanze* did not aspire to homely pretensions. It was a functional space, willed into existence in a forest between mountains, where the Führer fretted and didn't listen and yelled and imposed his will. There was no knowing then that Rommel and Paulus toiled in blazing North Africa and icy Stalingrad, years apart, while their Führer walked the woods, fidgety and burdened, that he knew what I didn't: that victory was elusive, uncertain.

When she did talk, mutter to herself, Marie whispered something almost incoherent about diesel shortages infuriating top commanders, about the war being that of survival rather than victory. Was she an eavesdropper? In fact, she said, sobbing, the war was possibly already lost, that all would, in time, be discovered. Every ghastly scene, every unmistakeable record, thefts of varied kinds; that all the sordid secrets and excesses would eventually be laid bare. She talked to me without addressing me, mumbling to herself, and because I did not know whether she had been sent to spy, refrained from even the slightest response. Not a word.

So she kept quiet and, turned away from me, cupped bath water with her palms and onto her back, a momentary flash of the sides of her breasts seen from under her armpits as she lifted her hands to rain water on the crown of her head, moist breast glimpsed in dim light, breast whose nipples I wasn't brave enough to touch, breasts whose faces remained a mystery to me. Yes, nipples are the faces of breasts; they set the tone, determine the very nature of the breast, its stance, how it demands to be viewed, its rebellion against time. Because she was a lady or simply because she was modest, Marie always bathed with her back to me and, on stepping out of the bath, crossed her arms over her breasts thus concealing their faces. Her lower torso was left bare, the hairy shrine between her legs, those exemplary legs, the perfectly proportioned hips, her apple-form bottom and the black hair that ran half the length of her elaborate back, in rich, wet, curly strands.

I suppose I have always been a gentleman, or at least aspired to be, for I found I could not sustain even a few seconds of staring at her; that my gaze weakened, my head bowed, my face flustered with shame and suspended desire. I did on one occasion, however, notice one thing: the bath water had turned red, which prompted Marie to drain it, hurriedly dry herself and leave. One benefit of war was the conflicting sharpening and blunting of the senses. My nose could detect scents and smells associated with danger or relief, and picking up the smell of blood, in whatever variation, seemed second nature, an instinct that meant staying alive; the same way the clean and harmless smell of fresh sausages and vegetables so assaulted my nostrils that it left me in a state of tearful euphoria, my chest heaving with gratitude. It was a scent that overshadowed that of smoke and diesel fumes, of torched buildings and bodies, the imagined smell of morphine, sweaty and weary infantrymen marching up steep slopes, of ground soaked with dew, gunpowder from rattling machine guns, the elusive smell of fear and knotted bowels, the stink of wet socks in wet boots. There were other smells, of course: festering wounds, raging salty seas off Omaha Beach, bad breath from comrades; and the memory of smells from home: fried eggs at the breakfast table, crushed apple cores between the teeth, my young wife Elisabeth's musty armpits moments before sunrise.

I must have been doing a good job polishing those boots because although no one ever complimented me, not a soul complained. I continued polishing them on freezing mornings, under overcast skies, in light drizzles, to hold on to sanity. My boot polishing was a trance of sorts, an escape from my tattered conscience, guilt laden at being captured and allowing myself to live in relative comfort while my compatriots wasted away in manholes and shallow graves. I was a child still, twenty-two, drafted into a war that seemed determined to last an eternity, a child who had until my first kill, my first murder on the battlefield, never aimed as much as a catapult at a squirrel, living or dead. My guilt cautioned me against myself, that I had hardened, that I would continue to harden, to live without the pleasure and sensation that gave life variety and charm, that my mind and character were ruined before they had formed, crystallised. All I had was my confinement without reasons or known purpose, my rations of sausages, and a nocturnal Marie who was a servant, a detached companion, and my obscure mirror of and window into the outside world.

The body, I learned, revolts against confinement, for even with relatively impressive creature comforts – a good bed, that deep bath and a heated room, a mirror, regular hot meals – life is as much an activity of a healthy body as it is of a healthy mind, and nothing can be worse than a carnivorous mind feasting on itself, a mind laden with dead ends and muted eruptions. I had an eerie feeling that I had entered a zone of discomfort, that there would be doubt and despair in whichever direction and, worse, that I might never be able to find a path to known and safe places.

So I polished boots, always ten pairs, never more, never less. The boots told me things: where their owners had walked, what relationship they had with bootlaces (three pairs were of picky, neat freaks, while most were of clumsy men who learned little from military code), and thus a glimpse into their souls. One boot had teeth marks on the nose, a suggestion or confirmation that a prisoner or some other unfortunate had been kicked in the teeth with such force that their teeth implanted permanent marks on the hardened leather; teeth that were clearly human teeth, not that of a dog or horse or goat. Some boots hinted, on occasions, at having patrolled on night missions – judging by the moths and night insects crushed underfoot. Some had visited women, as evidenced by strands of blonde or brunette hair lodged in the bootlaces, and inside one boot even a modest earring, a pinkish ruby encased in silver in need of polishing.

Something curious kept creeping up on me every time I sat on the veranda polishing boots: a veil of dust, fine dust, rained from the sky and onto the shiny boots with increasing frequency. On closer inspection, index finger swiping a small sample, I realised it was ash, evidence of burning, of something having been burned. I suspected it was because of the bombing raids, concrete ground to dust, leaving a powdery sediment. What, apart from a volcano, burned so intensely and with such scale as to rain ash on newly polished boots, on garden leaves, into coffee mugs left unattended? It was a futile curiosity, unimportant, not worthy of sleepless nights. Besides, wasn't ash just that – ash? Confirmation of an end to things by fire?

There were days when the ash was light, almost non-existent, but others when it seemed to hide the sun, though I couldn't always tell whether it was cloud cover or ash or both. The ash was at times a cheerful grey, the colour of light pigeons, but some mornings it fell in a dark, soot-like shade, the colour of sun-burned negro cooks, laundrymen and work mules caught in a war far removed from their aspirations.

The ash may even have fallen while I slept, while Germany slept, while the world slumbered. It continued falling on the polished boots and, if I forgot to cover them, into my coffee or food, turning my sausages a deathly grey. I wondered what would happen if I refused to polish the boots, if I rebelled, ignored them? Didn't my captors think I deserved some courtesy, that I at least deserved to know whose boots I was polishing? Wouldn't it be better if I were dragged kicking and screaming, lined up against the wall and shot?

Nothing seemed to be happening, or if it was, it was so minute – or so great – as to never be sensed or fully understood. There were days when Marie never showed up, days when there was no ash drizzling on polished boots or into my coffee, nights when the ground shook to an avalanche of bombs and tanks, mornings when my overgrown beard itched so badly that I had to scrape my face with the bottom of a boot. I realised with time that Commandant Althaus' compliments of me being good mannered were not, strictly speaking, to my benefit: they were boundaries, cautions, expectations that I not get too comfortable.

So I enjoyed good coffee and sausages without shaving, willed myself to act against male nature by dismissing my aching yearning for Marie as a suicidal luxury, even when I got so aroused that my toenails throbbed. Like a hound I salivated, increasingly unable to avert my gaze, as Marie bathed and muttered to herself, her back, worthy of the moonlight that passed through the window and bounced off it, birthing an image that could only be of an aquatic goddess. There were times, few, when I thought it cowardly to keep resisting the dictates of nature as God intended – that is, pretending I was unschooled in what would happen to me if Marie uncrossed her arms during her baths, if she stopped giving me her back, dared me with a frontal assault of her youthful breasts, breasts that by my sensory calculations would nestle perfectly in my blazing palms. Whereas innocents and the aged are immune and indifferent to the torments of carnal sieges, my times and age as an infantryman worked against all known restraints of remaining carnally sane. I was a sausage-fed, neurotic boot polisher wallowing in desire. I was not, however, what you would call a broken man – far from it, as I was neither a boy nor a full-grown man with real problems and life scars. It was that in-betweenness, that embryonic stage that was particularly disarming, that demanded answers to questions much greater than the questions themselves.

It was, on second thought, dangerously presumptuous that Marie found me worthy of sensual entrapment, friendship even. Whatever her thoughts of me, it was quite possible that she disliked me, even hated me, considering all the cleaning up after me without compensation. Maybe she pitied me, or looked through me; maybe her passions were invested elsewhere, in places and persons unknown. Weren't British and American bombers pounding Germany to ruins? What could possibly make me desirable, worth pursuing, when my countrymen rained death and mayhem on Berlin? Or was her hiding her breasts itself a subtle invitation? Of what kind? What if her nocturnal nudity, those baths of hers, were a language in themselves, a series of signals, codes, open-ended nudges that spoke in silence, torches that lit footpaths to desire? Or were they calls for help, urges for companionship, to belong? But again it was also quite possible that Marie thought very little about love or the war, that her discomforts predated food rations and aerial bombardments, that her burdens were of a personal and therefore private nature, that they had little or nothing to do with history or war or love, that history, love and war were in fact impediments to her attaining full bloom. Who was to say that those baths signified anything? Why wouldn't they have been simple hygiene rituals, cautions to the body against sweat and odours, attempts to revive a soul in distress?

There was no way of knowing then that every train, every boot, every scrap of paper, barbed wire and morsel of bread, every map and searchlight, every name on every list, every whisper and every pointing finger, siren and shovel, could be what burdened Marie, tainted her soul. It was every fly buzzing on every latrine, every sinew on bodies enslaved or free, every secret bunker, every hole and every attic, every railway line, every snarl and command, every fiery conscience and plotting mind that prompted those midnight baths. That with every sweep of that washcloth she sought to rid herself of the memory of every pill and bloody bandage, womb and pulsating heart, thought and doubt, wish and yearning, betrayal and discovery, every nail in every coffin, every boil on every face, every rat and roach in every camp, every speck of earth and ash, every culled hope, every bone fragment and every soup stain. That every squeeze of that sponge sought to wash away the thought of every maggot on every severed head, every stamp on every letter, every bloodstain on every wall, nipple on untouched breast, crucifix around the neck of every priest, bee in and out of blooming flowers, frostbite and futile prayer, every enraged and maddened poet confiding in every cynical prisoner. With her back to me she cleansed herself from the taint of every blind man who would never truly see the true horrors and evils of war rendered in freeze frames, every emissary and every prostitute, every vomit pail and every stolen Rembrandt.

Apart from summary executions, enslavement of the most imaginative kinds, it seemed to me that not all of Germany was at war. I had, on our motorcycle, train and car trips between Leipzig and Berlin and to Rastenburg, seen shell-shocked mothers pushing shivering babies in prams, old men staring forlornly at rubble, ruins of what used to be homes, remnants of butcher shops, even bomb craters in the middle of cemeteries – the dead were already dead and unable to wage war, and yet they too were bombed, out of their ancient graves, out of newer and fresh coffins.

I was very pleased but felt no less guilty of the fact that I had escaped the worst cold ever known, had a life of relative comfort imposed on me while my comrades were being blown to shreds on their grand march to Berlin. But the transition had not been without its own hell: I discovered that bones can be very temperamental things. Unbeknown to me, my bones had become used to freezing in the open fields, and the sudden access to sustained warmth made them ache so badly that I thought marrow would seep from my every orifice. I attempted to stop the pain by changing sleeping positions every five minutes – foetal with hands between my knees, flat on my belly, on my knees with buttocks in the air – to ease what felt like a hundred hammers crushing bone. I could feel the pain approach, as if from a faraway province, a dot on the horizon, slowly creep closer, drop hints, embed itself in every nerve end, and with determined ease, like starving lions, start licking at my carcass before the hammer blows began. I thought it was because of the cold; I had no way of knowing for certain.

I also suffered my fair share of fevers, and sudden access to good food was not without earth-moving vomiting and chronic diarrhoea, so much so that I couldn't help but laugh at myself, laughter that was at first embarrassing, then carefree, bordering on demented.

Did Roosevelt ever think of me, I wondered. Did he think of any of us, or did he sit in that wheelchair of his signing executive orders? Did he know how cold the German winter could be, that the chill of the Ardennes Forest sometimes made me wish someone would put a bullet through my skull? Did someone whisper to him that I was missing, and if someone did, was he prepared to make his way to the heart of the Reich, seek me out, bang on tables and demand I be released at once? Would he understand that I had ceased to be young, that I was an aged spirit, that my youthful looks were a sham, that they had nothing to do with beauty or innocence or promise, that they were a shell, a pit, an eternal sandstorm, a mockery of the civilisation we were supposedly fighting for, a distraction from painful truths? That in that supposed handsomeness tarnished by sausages lay a fathomless wasteland, so ancient but as yet not fully formed, a youth denied its nature, its natural rhythms, thrust into a world of old men and their ambitions, their nightmares.

There were, in that bewilderment, memories that refused to fade, how we, on our entry to Sainte-Mère-Église, lost Private Hansberry, one of our finest snipers. He was shot in the hip, a serious but not necessarily fatal wound, one that needed no more than a teaspoon of compassion and care. We let him die. None of us would touch nigger blood. The cheerful Private Hansberry with skin like black grapes, who sang like forty angels. I wonder what he, as he lay dying, thought of America, of Roosevelt, of me. Was it sufficient stroking his hair, wool textured like a house broom, as we watched him fade, bleed into the cold ground, get glassy-eyed and become motionless. It seemed that because it was not designed, not expected to be forgiving, war allowed for all sorts of blanket perversions, contortions of the soul, contradictions.

Marie had disappeared for a day, and returned hysterical. She ran the bath, stripped and clambered in, her hands still trembling. And for the first time in ninety days something happened. Something. She did not cross her arms across her chest, but let them slump at her sides, her breasts in full bloom. She scrubbed herself harder than ever, as if besieged by termites, as if she had insects crawling all over her. She wept silently, despaired, and in broken English intimated that she had seen things, smelled things, heard mouthfuls without a single word having been uttered.

It was during this rambling that I got to know that Marie Amsel was born on 24 August, in Leipzig, to a family of artisans. Cobblers. Motor mechanics. Builders. Because of a sick cousin, a boom in industry and a nascent culture scene, the eighteen-year-old Marie joined her mother, Susana, who worked as a nurse in Berlin in the summer of 1933. She insisted on spending a full month – between August and September – in Berlin, as a wobbly dancer at the *Tanztheater*. An ankle injury recast her ambitions as a tea lady at the *Berliner Tageblatt* and later as a trainee photographer – one who often forgot her tea obligations.

She, while on a nervous date with a certain Sebastian, a cerebral grandson of the newspaper editor, photographed a dying horse. It was that one photograph, with the horse twitching in a sea of autumn leaves, the sun dipping behind a giant maple, the light goldish and soft, the horse's hindquarters in mid-air, mane blown by a breeze, that recast her future as a photographer. The image was framed as a giant portrait at the newspaper offices, with a Mozart quotation that read: 'I thank God for graciously granting me the opportunity of learning that death is the key to our true happiness.' It was followed years later by dazzling documentary images of rallies of National Socialist German Workers' Party, cemeteries, street scenes, religious rituals and visiting jazz ensembles.

PLEASURE

Her growing body of work eventually gave her unprecedented access to important people, people some only heard on the radio, saw in newspapers, at important government events. She met, shook hands with and photographed Paul von Hindenburg, Leni Riefenstahl, Goebbels, Göring, Eichmann and a host of other notables, from commandants to poets, and having shot factories, cityscapes, military parades and suchlike, became entrusted in an official capacity with photographing, recording important events, rare sights, interesting things. In reality, nothing had really changed. She remained a photographer as she had always been, had the same aura of a famous and celebrated artist; only the world around her had changed, was changing, crystallising into sights she never imagined. The lens that had immortalised a dying horse burdened her, soiled her, stoned her heart, buried her alive. She was dirtied by war, compelled to scrub herself bloody as she tried to set herself free, divorce herself from tailing Eichmann's Angels as they swept from camp to camp. Treblinka. Sobibór. Bełżec. Dachau. Auschwitz-Birkenau. Chełmno. Others. As dentists smashed jaws with hammers, hacked at bridges to extract crowns, gold teeth, she knew even then, through her camera, at Goebbels' behest, where all that ash came from. She knew why the skies darkened, saw the fires that raged in camps and outlying fields as Eichmann's trains kept coming, ferrying the gaunt and the condemned, who like cattle herded to an abattoir sensed all was not well, without having exact words to articulate their suspicion.

So smoke and ash rose, the ash falling onto polished boots and into coffee and onto sausages, and Marie soaked in her midnight baths. It was amazing that people worked that hard, collecting firewood, digging furnaces, moving mountains of the stiff, starved, only to be consumed by fire, said Marie. Then, she had to, when the day was done, deal with the frisky and sweaty palms of powerful men exploring her back, her waistline, her rump. One never knew how to react or what to say in such instances, she confided, how to feel, for though still a violation, she had witnessed countless SS men have their way with so many other terrified and apologetic women, who in exchange for safety, for belonging, for life, pawned their bodies to aged, turkey-necked men with dirty fingernails, pouchy bellies and foul breath. One's profession, one's reputation, one's standing in society did not matter, she said. Some chose to leer at you, no doubt make lewd jokes out of earshot, sparking raucous laughter among their comrades, laughter that left you enraged but completely defenceless. Isolated.

These men had wives, or histories with wives, rendezvous with mistresses and cheap skirts known to revel in social displays in their colourful garments and loud make-up, those with loud and shrieking laughter, skilled in weighing the promise and true worth of men. And it was precisely because of this that these holders of power expected all women to be uncomplicated, to embrace every grope, every stare, to accept that men have unpalatable natures. And, as such, women – even if young and respectable and daring – should understand that their lives were entangled with those of men who could, without forewarning or good reason, suddenly declare that a woman be taken to some cemetery some place, made to grab hold of a headstone, skirt lifted to her waistline, panties yanked aside, and be ravaged from behind. Or, in some instances, old men who, without saying a word, continued to be shifty, to steal glances when you were not looking, to often say: 'I wish I was younger.'

And it gets worse, she confided, for there is a difference in being a woman during times of peace and of war. Peace times can, as life is, be ruthless of course, but the ruthlessness of war means that there is no expectation of common decency to others, more so to women, so your entire existence is about survival, cunning, the loss of all things delicate. There are no norms in war, she added reflectively. Maybe uncertainty. Cruelty, certainly. Fear. Doubt. But no norms. I would rather be pointing my lens at bees courting flowers, at wedding couples, even fountains in public squares, but all that possibility is wasted on documenting strife. You cannot look at my photographs, she said, without being numbed, overwhelmed, violated. There is a certain misplaced feeling: that of dirt that just won't wash off. Dirt engrained in the soul. I should never have stopped being a dancer, never left Leipzig. Look at me now, she said. What have I become?

It was laughable that I fretted about dying, for if truth be told I felt, on the best of days, that portions of my soul had died the moment I shot that German tank commander who, in flames, begged for his life in the most beseeching, calmest, and evocative voice he could master: wide eyed, grovelling, mercy gestures and all. He even bowed to me, six times, imploring me not to kill him. He had forgotten that a war had been declared, that we were in the fiercest moments of that war, and that we were, by virtue of our uniforms, our orders, not in the business of nursing friendships or pitying remorseful and outgunned enemies. Our orders were to take Saint-Lô. How were we to do that if I allowed myself to be swayed by a soldier who had, by all indications, simply run out of bullets? He knew as well as I did that he would have, if he could, pulled that trigger without blinking, and yet he was expecting me to be merciful. I shot both his knee caps off, waited for his heightened prayers or curses, and when none came, shot him though the left hand, counted forty-three seconds, lit a cigarette, and shot him in the head. I was accused of being a savage, a sadist, of wasting valuable ammunition.

I was sitting on the veranda, polishing boots, when someone crept up on me from behind, unnoticed, unheard.

'I think the war is already lost,' he said. 'What do you think about that?'

'I wouldn't know,' I answered turning around.

'Can't comment or won't comment?'

I kept quiet.

'It is already lost … The relentless bombardments. War on multiple fronts. Our pitiful show in Stalingrad. The diesel shortages. War fatigue. Our incredibly impulsive Führer. I say we place a bet to confirm what I am saying; that the war is already lost. I know a farmer, a dear friend – pigs and sheep and things – who is very skilled with a knife. Whoever loses the bet loses their testicles under Frederich's knife. Nice clean wound, then a squat over a bucket for the initial gush of blood, add coarse salt to the wound. What do you say ... think?'

I was mute, then countered: 'It doesn't have to be that way. You are a wise man, Commandant, I am sure you speak with good authority from your invaluable experience with these matters. I am just a kid.'

'*Kind?*' he snorted. 'Is there no blood on your hands? You see, good manners can only take you so far, after which you have to own up to a few tragic but necessary truths, some of which might not be to your liking. I have men dying by their thousands in the frontline – some of whom consider themselves children, as you are so quick to point out. That is why we must commit to the ultimate sacrifice – castration – to show that we, as men, understand the gravity of our contribution to ruins here and elsewhere. That we elect to live the rest of our lives without wants, urges, the divine gift of siring offspring with hands red and sticky from taking the lives of others. It is logical, no?'

I went cold at the realisation that I was surrounded by men whose minds knew no limits, consciences decapitated from their thoughts; that they could think anything, will anything into being. In a split second, he decided he would, without my consent, commit my manhood to a pig farmer, complete with wound-care considerations, insights into coarse salt on butchered manhood.

Commandant Althaus looked into a distance, scratched the back of his head and added: 'War is futile, serves no one but itself. There will always be something to bear arms for. Conflict, it seems, is part of our nature as humans, no?' I nodded; he smiled, continued: 'There is a rumour that Roosevelt has a *wunder* bomb, the mother of all bombs, to end all wars. What do you know about that? The Führer wants to know. It is hard to believe that there could be a bomb worse than what we already know, have seen, experienced even.'

I don't know anything about any wonder bomb, I told him; that would be something confided only to senior generals. He chuckled, 'Fate is a cruel but fair master. Can you imagine if our Führer had such a weapon? How would you feel about that?'

I answered with silence, feeling somewhat betrayed that I knew only what Roosevelt wanted me to know. For all our valour, our nervous crawling through thick vegetation, our cautious sidestepping of booby traps, our witnessing of shredded bodies dangling from tree branches, or heads with gaping mouths severed from the bodies, tongues still attempting to mouth words, we knew nothing. But Roosevelt depended on spy planes and eavesdropping to know what Stalin and the Führer did not want him to know – what they selected he should know – and yet, despite that limited, incomplete and misleading knowledge, still sent men to their deaths by their millions.

It was only on his fourth visit that my captor, Commandant Althaus, disclosed – to his own rage and embarrassment – that there had been a terrible misunderstanding; that the man they sought was in all probability *not* me, that it was impossible that it was or could be me; that though good-mannered, I lacked the drive, the alertness, the gravitas of knowing the name and rank of *the man* they were seeking – some bomb expert I supposed –

whom they planned on capturing and torturing to death if the need arose. Such a man was rumoured to have commanded my platoon in Saint-Lô in the weeks leading up to my capture; the man who would lead the Panza Division to their man – the one whose name and rank I never learned.

I sighed. Another lesson: though we marched to the same beat, under the same flag, apparently on the same mission, it became apparent that not all of us were merely soldiers, that there were amongst us some with tentacles that stretched far and wide, invisible webs that connected them to important and valuable people, people with dark and heavy secrets. I was a pawn, a fool, bulging from sausages and unearned leisure, oblivious to weighty matters that determined the nature and duration of the war. They would have – could still – whipped, tortured and starved me, interrogated me about the bomb, yanked out my toenails with a pair of pliers, and I would not, in all honesty and pain inflicted, have managed to utter a single word worth their effort. I could have been hanged or shot or enslaved and still not yielded anything. So I trudged around in my SS uniform – the height of mockery – and polished boots, and unbeknown to me, drank the remains of the disabled, Honorary Aryans without documentation, Polish, Russians, Hungarians, Ukranians, 'Rhineland Bastards', Sorbs, Czechs, Jews and gypsies in my coffee.

Marie claimed that someone had tried to kill the Führer and failed. Someone had tried to blow to pieces the supreme leader of the Third Reich while he studied battle maps. I was so close, on the very premises, yet so far from that awkward man who, as Marie said, walked on some mornings, attended to military affairs until 2 pm, then lunched, before retiring to a love-starved Eva Braun, all the while thinking only of world domination.

Poor Eva: love sick while the Führer was present, but even then still absent – lost in thought, mentally digging foxholes, erecting barbed-wire perimeters, positioning snipers, shipping supplies, studying terrains and battlefields, establishing from where waves and positions of resistance could or should be expected. All the time, every waking moment, he would be estimating distances, gathering intelligence, marshalling troops, double checking with command centres, being briefed by bombardiers, studying aerial photographs, signing declarations. In his addled mind he would be constructing bunkers, imposing food rations, nodding at grave diggers, moving tanks, shaking the hands of historians, the odd gala dinner to give an air of normality. And, with all that, he failed to hear her legitimate request: 'Please … Please, my Führer, come to bed.'

I do not want to be like Eva, said Marie. She is not as happy as she seems: riding the bicycle, filming the Führer with that irritating camera she points at everything. I don't think the Führer loves her; that he is in fact capable of loving anyone, and even if he does, it is a strange kind of love: without tenderness, devoid of passion, stripped of romance. It seems to me that he loves the dogs more than he does her. There is a momentary glint in his eyes when he brushes the dogs, like he *himself* were one with them, a beast; and yet that sparkle is absent when he plays with even the most cheerful of children. It's a sham, all his bowing and smiling at little ones, asking them silly questions. I don't think he has it in him to love, to truly surrender to the comforts and thrills of love. He thrives in discomfort, has always thrived in solitude, will always be unaffected. How do some people achieve that: the detachment, the indifference, the otherworldly, head-in-the-clouds resolve? It is all his fault. His and that Desert Fox of his …

They took him away from me, you know … Buried him in North Africa, in desert sand, the same sand where Montgomery's men emptied their pails, swarming with waste and flies. So young, so handsome, so calm spirited, drafted into a war and then shot within three days of arrival. No letter, no message; just a void, a cold shadow of what might have been. My poet and birdwatcher with ruby lips, who was incapable of raising his voice. Alois. That was my fiancé's name. An unmarked grave. That birdwatcher, who was fascinated by printing presses, how ink smeared onto rolls of paper, how pictures of people and things married newspapers and magazines at high speed; how the smell of ink, pungent but tolerable, had the potential to birth news, commit love and poetry to paper. Ink, said Alois, was the surest measure to create records, issue commands, court eternity. Thirsty and dehydrated, gritting desert sand between his teeth, the Führer had with a stroke of a pen committed Rommel to lead the Aloises of the world to their graves. Alois, who prayed with eyes open, staring far into the distance, had a reputation for the funniest yet heartfelt prayers that to the less discerning bordered on the blasphemous.

The Führer is gone – to Chancellor House, back to Berlin. They are coming, said Marie, her brow furrowed. They have outrun all German defences. Stalin's boys. Churchill's. Americans. Commandant Althaus is dead. Someone identified him as a conspirator, as too eager to surrender, to take power. The Führer ordered that he be arrested and executed. What will happen to you now, she asked.

I don't remember what happened to Marie, but recall dreaming, quite vividly, of stumbling across a vast field of ruins towards a sunrise; only the sun was rising sideways, drizzling ash as it trekked along the horizon. A cloud of dust rose sky high, painting a blurry, blackening picture from the core of which, across a partially bombed bridge, emerged tanks flanked by cheering and jubilant Russians. In my dream I shrugged off my SS uniform and, unsure, in the nude, walked toward the advancing tanks. The house phone rang, woke me from my bathtub slumber – the water icy, the skin on my fingertips and toes wrinkled like dried prunes – into the present, to the sea hinting at uncouth behaviour, sending an insolent breeze through the fluttering curtains, to the rumble of distant thunder.

The Remington

There is pleasure, but no pleasure in teaching. Teaching is not what it used to be. I admit to being a hopeless teacher, lacking in instincts required for worthwhile inquiry. I tolerate my students, fake interest in encrypted information: *Vagabonds in the Novels of VS Naipaul: A Historic Analysis*. I have no stomach for it and only persist because I would artistically starve to death without it, this peeping into cultures and civilisations, this chore called academia. All that lay between me and artistic destitution is this pantomime of being a professor who, in the world's eyes, has no regard for such elevations.

My students? I reward the wise and interesting, tolerate average minds, skip scheduled appointments with the slow and stupid. I dish out notes, bulk assignments, point my hounds sniffing into Foucault's toils, and disengage. I am often accused of being too arm's-length, not involved, of abusing the refuge of sabbaticals. I burden Professor Beaudrie with my flock, flatter her in guarded ways, until I am safely perched in front of Father's

Remington. It gives me great pleasure being free, to sleep without alarm clocks or read stuffy essays on Post Modernism. I pretend not to hear the condemnations, whispers meant to be heard, to hurt, as Ambrosia – the dimmest in my flock – accuses me of laziness. The cheerful 'Good morning, Prof!' Or 'Here comes Plato,' have been replaced by throaty grumbles, insults I pretend not to hear: 'The dictator asshole with a blunt red pencil.' Abella is, unlike me, a natural, a capable teacher patient with even the slowest of minds.

Months of daydreaming pass, of strange dreams in the bath or on the couch, but none as colourful as that of Marie and Commandant Althaus, months in which very little or no work is done. All I ever wanted to be is a great writer – as great as my father, if not much greater. What has crippled my manuscript, denied it life, is the eventual realisation that although carnal pleasure dominates human lives, it is by no means the only one. Yet its powerful pull distorts this reality, that it is not the only one, thus reducing other pleasures to a small letter *p*. It is possible that Marie's midnight baths, her nudity, were not complete in themselves, and could only truly be appreciated in conjunction with an acknowledgement of the elusiveness of the steam that rose from her bathwater, the aroma of coffee in the moonlight, even the simple pleasure of falling asleep in a comfortable bed, with the shaky knowledge that no one – even in a dream – was going to shoot you. The possibilities of love and courtship were themselves pleasurable; the knowledge that

Marie's beloved was rotting in the desert sands of North Africa, the perverse assumption that there was little or no competition in wooing her heart.

There was, of course, the pleasure of Marie as housekeeper – cleaning, overseeing culinary matters, bringing boots for polishing – which, though awkward, meant I, as Giovanni Gomez, did not have to worry about making my own bed. It is astonishing how a mindless chore like that occupies a mind and, its being assigned to Marie meant I could use those eight seconds to turn my thoughts to my aching bones, the mysterious ash, about what it was like to be Rommel. Such little freedoms also gave me a moment to think about Elisabeth, my young bride, whom I had not spoken to or touched in months; to remember her scones, her timid but kind nature, the embarrassment with which she battled her cluelessness in the arena of most matters sensual, cluelessness cultivated and plastered by the Church with threats of hell and eternal damnation, that sensations, awarded at birth, were the devil's work; that desire – even the thinking of it – was sinful.

Was it possible, as Giovanni Gomez or even Milton, to divorce myself from Marie, who aroused and confused me, saved me from the ice that chilled my bones? I was right there in the snow, walking among ruins, polishing boots. I felt the sting of the cold, smelled the mortar rounds, got shot at on Omaha Beach. I was there, and I have been gifted this story to pick apart, to weigh, to assemble. Why then don't the puzzles fit? I have been given a story, beginning to end, of Giovanni, of Marie and her midnight baths, but I cannot say which of its components are weighty enough for Father's Remington. Should it be a tale of war, of love, or sensuality or dying? It does not help that Father was such a natural in these matters, at sifting diamonds from crystallised mud. Maybe it was *just* a dream, no different from someone dreaming of flying a kite or kissing their boss; not a story at all. There is perhaps nothing to be learned from it. Maybe it is just documentaries of 1945 embedded in memory: nothing more. But did it, if it was a dream, have to be so vivid, so real, so *felt*? Giovanni or not, that snow, the cold, that ash raining into my coffee, those boots I polished, Marie's exemplary back *were* real!

But again – as yet another soaking session in the bath led me to believe, with the promise of some substance at last, but not certainty – my attempts failed because I, unlike talented but reckless poets, simply had not lived enough, did not possess enough life experience to illuminate life's dark alleys. That much I learned from Rilke, who as my companion when cleaning my parents' graves and dabbling in poetry in the shade, said: 'Make use of whatever you find about you and express yourself, the images from your dreams and the things in your memory. If your everyday life seems to lack material, do not blame it; blame yourself, tell yourself that you are not poet enough to summon up its riches; for there is no lack for him who creates and no poor, trivial place.' That's Rainer Rilke in *Briefe an einen Jungen Dichter*. Do I lack material, even when Giovanni and Marie have presented it to me on a silver platter?

I think pleasure evades touch, without trying. Its essence, the cemetery shade assured me, is not anything profound, but a realisation that pleasures are coded from birth, are divine gifts to living things without expectation or complicity, without prior arrangements on how the pleasures should be possessed and sampled – whether in cerebral or physical preoccupations, as gateways to things radiant and spiritual. Pleasure coexists with strife, mirrors yearning. But how does one write all these observations, some without conclusive proof, in a way that is not self-indulgent, circular, for the selfish reasons of literature? Maybe, I think to myself, the presence of doubt is the ruin of my premise; it drowns me, blunts me, hands me fading torches. How did Father manage, how did he ignore the uncertainties of literature? If I had told him my dream, handed both Giovanni and Marie to him, dared him to do what he wished with them, what would he have omitted, suggested, put on a pedestal? Would he not have touched *pleasure* at all, elected instead to write about the indifference of snow, the futility of war, the significance of ash? Because he could be stubborn, so unyielding, it is quite possible that he could have listened with interest but without commitment, and proceeded to write a tome about a clingy writer son. One never knew with Father, how that mind of his worked, how it found depth in the most negligible of things: bird migrations, the sixty seconds that make a minute, even blood that stains the odd egg shell. He would have asked, sternly, why I was not considering Africa and her place in the universe, instead of courting vague themes. I would not have answered him, not immediately, or would have done so only in non-committal ways, ways that – like my reflections – remained deeply felt but elusive. Why couldn't I transcend myself, the continent, engage in the beautiful and the speculative? Who is to say that Mateusz, Franciszek and Adamina despised Africa, if one never spoke to them? If pleasure blankets the universe, was given generously and with no heed to borders, to a species: why shouldn't empathy and grief and mourning and desire not be extended to Marie, to Antoni, Albinka and seventeen million others? My manuscript is ruining me, but I do not know how.

Wouldn't it have been better to be a carpenter, driving nails into wood with sure and tangible results, instead of thinking in circles, driving myself mad? Why be a writer when one can own a nightclub and marvel at drunken revellers dance, or a daring inventor inspired to build a rocket with which to journey to the sun? What is this obsession with literature, with what things mean and how? I take a sip of the wine, three gulps in one to empty the bottle. I can smell the sting on the fermented grapes escape through my nostrils, as I rest my head on a towel, and think: what is pleasure? Perhaps, I think, the Marie Dream was nothing more than a courting of the essence. But why then was it contaminated by such misery? If Marie was a proxy, a stand-in for its scope and variations, how was it that pleasure approached me via such an obscure route: wartime 1945? The connections are puzzling, impossible to detect, and yet I feel there are clues in this entanglement of possibilities: finding and confirming what they are, their true fire, would mean I had something, however meagre, to say to the Remington. How did Father, with a past like a stained mirror, undesirable, peel into the core of things: the hospitals without drugs, job seekers resorting to eating out of garbage bags, starting history on a clean page? How would I present pleasure as Father would, with arm's-length intimacy? I feel incapable of taming that Remington. It taunts me, dares me, asks: what do you *know* about pleasure? What do you know that is worth sharing?

I am not like my father; I fiddle, suffer false thoughts, overestimate my capabilities. He would have sat in silence, in the shadows – sunrise, sunset, twilight – plotting a way into the puzzle, consuming coffee, waiting for a thread, a pattern to become apparent. I find I am hasty, impulsive, more suited to a life of modest leanings than rumination that would lead to the creation of profound things.

But my problems are not merely literary, I must hasten to add. One by one, for different reasons of varying complexity, my lovers left me: first Professor Beaudrie, then Masechaba, followed by Alexis. I know that it is not possible to compare the varied and soul-warming pleasures I enjoyed from three hearts that throbbed for me for so many years, against their doubts and anger and silent bidding, through my every indecision and boyish antics. There is nothing worse than a grown man who has little respect for time, who assumes it will always be there, that he owns his time and that of others; that those who love him don't change, have no further aspirations, that their lives revolve around his. My loneliness has a heaviness to it, stuffiness, a dimness that distorts time and feeling to such unknowable degrees that it is futile trying to question or understand any of it.

Time has lapsed now, rendered the past distant but still elusive. My loves are married; Alexis to a banker and Masechaba I don't know who, as she divorced the red-bearded *South Africa Live* newscaster who reads us news about Muammar Gaddafi, the cost of oil per barrel and drug busts at Heathrow. I attended both Alexis' and Masechaba's weddings, but never imagined that 'You may now kiss the bride' could have such finality, be such a wounding granting of marital rights. Both sent me wedding pictures in which I look dazed and on the brink of tears. They call me once in a while, leave long messages on voicemail, about all the wonderful opportunities I let pass, assure me that I will always be loved, and when in distress, ask me to decode 'men stuff' when their husbands act out of character. Alexis: 'You think he's having an affair?', 'Should I lose some weight? Be honest!' or 'How should I manage his overly sensitive ego?' Professor Beaudrie spent a month lecturing in Le Mans and sent two or three postcards, the themes of which dwelt on the works of French existentialist writers, Western philosophers. A Blaise Pascal card read, 'There is no better proof of human vanity than to consider the causes and effects of love, because the whole universe can be changed by it. Cleopatra's nose.' And Nietzsche affirming Pascal with, 'The demand to be loved is the greatest of all arrogant presumptions.'

Losing all three is unbearable and my loss has carved a hole in my being, and yet, as hard as I try, I cannot convince myself that I was ever ready to commit to any one of them. I have written and abandoned countless manuscripts – prose, verse, letters – in an attempt to quantify all the pleasures I have enjoyed with my three beloveds: their culinary surprises, laughter and tears at fights and emotional reconciliations, the distinct temperatures and sleeping patterns of all three bodies, their divergent but strangely complementary personalities (playful, secretive and the nurturer), their intensities in voicing displeasure, and the manner and timing of their small deceits. But I remain the greatest deceiver of them all in having thought that full disclosure, white lies to maintain perspective, would stall time, suspend aspirations, suspend the laws set by nature. The sum total of pleasures lost and gained in those years is immense; known pleasures, great pleasures, but even the minutest of them: how each knocked on the door with charm or anger, their treatment of pillows during and after sleep, and for smoker Beaudrie the slight tilting of the head when she lit a cigarette; the terrifying pleasure of not knowing when the next pleasure would come or what form it would take, that I might not be alive to meet it; how each laughed and begged for mercy when tickled (I am an unrepentant tickler: soles of feet, armpits, earlobe nibbler); the way they narrated their dreams; forgetful Alexis' countless smiles and, my God, how she cut toasted bread into small squares; Beaudrie's dancing to club music in her panties.

It seems to me now that I was always going to fail in my toils for a revelatory manuscript because my very existence, my being, is – as pointed out by Rilke – one of half-measures. This is not to say I'm unaware of this predicament, but where to begin in nudging it closer to the fire, setting it alight in the hope of examining the ashes, recording its transformations? I am convinced a tome on pleasure is still possible, that with the right cast, the right script, with proper lighting, clues might emerge and thus dramatise pleasure in ways that are proving elusive on Father's Remington. Or maybe I am too hasty, too eager to lead, to set a tone. It is quite possible, of course, that all pleasure is doing is exhausting me, draining me, weaning me of all half-truths and then taking me by the hand to an ocean shore under a starry night somewhere, pointing at constellations above and saying: 'I am everywhere, not on typewriter keys. I detest measurements, for my form is formless, my nature silent. You don't laugh or exclaim or muse in pleasure as you have so concluded. I am sorry to tell you that by the time you remember all things pleasant, doubt your intentions, dream colourful and memorable things, whisper things into the ears of lovers, leaving them giddy and enchanted, the second you become aware that there's a possibility I could be there, be courted, I am *already* long gone. I am there before you perceive I will be; I cast shadows, leave a faint scent and, by the time you wonder if I would be your friend, I would have long marked you, pointed you to vast possibilities with rusty *No Trespassing* signs at locked gates. A word of advice: why don't you write about the war, touch on *my* shadows in it? Not me. Give the Remington a break. Your fingers will be scarred, bleed, fall off. I admit I exist, but I am never truly there so as to permit gravestones and memorials, allow hand holding of any kind. If it makes you feel better, your father knew this. Why do you think he never attempted?'

I miss the irritants that come with intimacies: accidental burps, morning breath determined to rewrite definitions of 'foul', daring sleeping positions; Abella lighting up, painting the room with cloud webs, completely nude, and in the most detached of voices complaining, subtly accusing me of eyeing the ever-cheerful and leggy Monica from Little Bombay.

'You fancy other women. I see your roving eye when you think I am not looking. What is it with you and women?'

I kept silent, planted miniature kisses along her ribs.

'Are we trophies to you, me and the others, others I might never know, spoils of war, of history? This goes beyond manly appetites, doesn't it – you stalking the finest among us, helping yourself as if in revenge? And revenge for what exactly? Why do I feel this way, that I am a curiosity, a conquest, a pastime? I have this strange, empty, and sickening feeling that I am some trophy for you, little else, and often wonder if I mean anything to you, if I matter, or worse, if you even think of me at all the second my legs are closed. I feel traces of your love, don't get me wrong, minute twitches, yet somehow too little to alter and erase this deep longing and expectation to be loved and felt and cherished by you. Is that too much to ask? It pains me that it seems I lack something, that I possess in me a rift that will never be filled, that I am one to be stalked and encircled, pounced upon, devoured, then gently discarded for other vultures to rip through my rotting carcass, unsightly debris no longer of any value. How long will it take for me and my kind to pay for century-old sins so that we may be seen as whole people, not just sewers through which the horrors of history flow?'

Over and above its expansive view of the sea, the sea with all its charms and fury, Casablanca Estates is nestled between a chain of sea-facing hotels, and at street level, an assortment of restaurants and curio shops swarming with camera-laden tourists. It is not uncommon to hear Spanish, French, Italian or Mandarin and, on some Thursdays, to see displays of traditional dance from bare-breasted Africans with ready smiles. There is the wider Cape Town metropolis, of course, pregnant with history and memorials and scenery and racism, with multimillion-rand addresses in gated-off suburbs and on cliffs, but the immediate vicinity of Casablanca Estates is the preserve of that constant rumbling of the ocean, of lonely housewives stealing glances at strangers, poetry Tuesdays at Poets Abode next to the ice-cream parlour, and two blocks further, seafront coffee and book shops, colour contrasts from an assortment of street-parked vehicles, and six blocks further along the seashore the Culture Institute, and yet a few paces to the east, a five-minute drive, the Little Bombay restaurant on a leafy avenue.

From Father's apartment, which I have now stripped of almost all his possessions, except the writing table, that spine-breaking chair and that torturous Remington, one can, from behind the burgundy curtains, smell the sea in all its saltiness and mystery, catch the wail of ships' sirens as they approach the harbour, jet engines slowing down en route to the airport. Behind the burgundy curtains, in the company of the echoes of my footstep, I imprison myself, compare myself to my double: the Milton slaving behind the Remington in a bare apartment up against the 1945 Giovanni Gomez under house arrest at the *Wolfschanze*; the now loveless Milton finding solace in the murmurs of the sea and that double in my dream besieged by Marie's pain, her midnight baths, her sensual otherworldliness. How could he possibly be Giovanni Gomez if such a grave crime could unfold under his very nose, yet still he made no attempt to learn more, did nothing but lust after Marie's breasts, a passive lust that yielded nothing?

Unlike Giovanni's plump-thighed and musty-pitted Elisabeth, all my former lovers, in their own distinct ways, were most exemplary in the realm of scent, offering an unparalleled pleasure, a feasting on inviting scent from warm, living, twitching flesh.

PLEASURE

How they sharpened my senses those early mornings – how they humanised me, dismantled and screwed me back together in the most profound and subtle ways and, with that constant friend, the sea, confirmed Father's fleeting lesson that literature is primarily an occupation of *feeling* and not thought.

Eagle-eyed I see and observe things, sense the minutest shifts, ponder connections and contrasts in lucid detail. Evidence of this lies in the frequency of the bell of that Remington, marking the speed of sentence after sentence as I sit pounding those keys in the nude. I completely lose track of time as I wallow through heartbreaks I have seen and known, those going on at street level below Casablanca Estates: all these people so full of life and yet in the process of dying. What great pretence there is in knowing we are born to die, somehow and eventually, but unless afflicted by some dreaded disease or missed by a speeding car that knowledge, of death lurking everywhere, allow that thought to remain dormant, insignificant even. Except for Marie. She – with her camera, tears, sighs and midnight baths – never for a moment let that thought slip from her consciousness. She did not organise protest marches, author rebellious pamphlets, set herself on fire, yet refused any form of complacency as to the destructiveness of the Führer. She, armed with a camera, without a single word of protest, stood her ground against the Allied forces crossing Ludendorff Bridge on the Rhine on their grand March to Berlin, before things got desperate, before the *Furher's Jeugen*, twelve-year-olds, got shot in the head.

I muse: maybe a man needs not love or pleasure, but truth …

I think: truth by the teaspoon from a faded black-and-white picture of rags belonging to perished prisoners.

I confirm: truth seeping from tear ducts, Marie mourning the potential of humans to be brutes.

I picture: truth on every rising and falling wave of the expansive sea, the sea viewed from behind burgundy curtains only fractionally and momentarily pulled aside, the sea connected to other seas, seas that sailed men, bombs and cargo.

I innumerate: the sea that, without raising its voice, drowned and swallowed what it chose, as and when it felt like it. Binoculars. Maps. Bullets. Whole ships. Dreams. Civilisations. Desires. Naval engineers. Disease that would inflict bodies years into the future. Fantasies. Incomplete Psalm 23s on the trembling mouths of the terror stricken and drowning. Misunderstandings captured in Morse code. American, British, German flags. Cooks with stewing pots obliterated by salty, freezing waters. War manuals.

I conclude: profounder truths about how, in the grander scheme of creation, minuscule human efforts are, how there remains even in their worst destructions, their greatest and mind-bending pleasures, a lack, a longing, obscurity.

As the Remington bell rings, with frequency and long pauses, reflections and confirmations, the sea, seen from the window of my false refuge, whispers assurances, prompts inquiry, withholds explanations. The same view that so enchanted Father – mined him, perhaps emptied him of words – confronts me in torrential downpours and mist, gale-force winds and overcast horizons, in heat waves, under starry nights, in the company of the setting sun or rising moon, both laying carpets of light, footpaths, on its calm face.

PLEASURE

I eat and sleep poorly; I work too much. Shipments of mail lie unattended on the study floor. What do they want? A quick, uninterested glance notes the familiar, branded envelopes: bank statements, utility bills, traffic violations, offers of bank loans – all of which have no bearing or contribution to the ring of that Remington bell. Two letters are from foreign universities, one American, the other Polish. I wonder what they want? Carlos Santana sings, once, twice, sometimes eight times a day, and each time I let calls divert to voicemail or the answering machine, which in turn records and deletes greetings, concerns, invitations, requests, accusations, propositions, seductions, confirmations, threats, appeals, and questions from an assortment of inquisitors as and when the machine's memory is filled. There are knocks at the door, many knocks, of various resolve and intensities, even in the oddest hours of night, knocks I pretend not to hear. There is no evidence of life in Apartment 4003, or at least I convince myself so, except that Remington and its bell. What proof does anyone have that it's *me* typing away? My door note should be a diversion enough: *In Johannesburg on Private Business. Date of Return Unknown.* It works – but only just. The gap at the bottom of the door is filling with notes, hastily scribbled, some with language bordering on threats. Abella's notes. One from Alexis. None from Marie. Because pleasures have standards, victims and purgatories, in hindsight it seems to me that woven with the quest for pleasure is a tacit contract to heartbreak. And yet there remains an important distinction to be made: that heartbreak, no matter how despotic or reckless, chooses its victims vigilantly and, unbeknown to them, corners them, herds them into dungeons from which they might never emerge. But as one shooting star, breaking rank with cosmic arrangement, that nocturnal heavenly design, does not rattle other stars from their positions so are the ways of pleasure. Like the mysterious birth and explosive deaths of stars, other pleasures will continue, others die, new ones invented, regardless of whether Abella and Alexis suffer. I will limp from my dungeon, flogged to despair, to reflect on what to make of this thing called life.

Part of the problem is this: I occasionally collect mail and subscriptions from my former matrimonial house on 66 Jasmine Road, not a palace but a comfortable place that is the result of honest labour: tiled driveway, automated gates, an immaculate garden, three-bedroomed, double-storeyed and painted grey with cherry accents, impressive palm trees, and that beloved, sun-facing balcony on which I devoured wartime poets. The house is in a good neighbourhood, not that of bankers and mining magnates, but decent enough to warrant modest pride, tinges of guarded nostalgia. I guess that that is to be expected when it comes to abandoned matrimonial nests: memories laced with relief and pathos, partly because the subscriptions managers at *Time* and *National Geographic* magazines do not care about the intricacies of a complicated life at 66 Jasmine Road. Neither do traffic departments and dentists' accountants who continue to send me reminders of driving and dental mishaps; or congratulatory letters from insurance companies announcing an increase in monthly premiums.

Last week Thursday was such a day, of letter sorting and awkward smiles, a day that should have ended innocently but didn't. I found Orapeleng – my ex-wife – in a cheerful mood, but on closer inspection was able to attribute that to a bottle of red wine from which at least two glasses had been poured, further evidence of which lingered on her breath as she tried to kiss me. I averted my head, with courtesy and dignity, I hope. She laughed it off, and right there in the living room, with John Coltrane tilting his saxophone at us from that prized painting of mine, the one she so vehemently denied should be taken down when I moved out, unzipped her skirt, let it drop to the floor, stood there with a coy smile.

'You, my love,' she continued, 'are not even a proper womaniser. You simply don't have the balls for it. Womanising is clinical, a ruthless business. You are not cut out for it. Never were. That is why you are so clumsy, amateurish, and over time I foresee worse disasters. Why don't we forget about all the stupid things past? Why don't you come home?'

I stuck my hands in my pockets, to regain composure, and maintained silence.

'Failing which, if you're keen, something that would be inadequate but better than nothing, we could simply be bed buddies. Friends with benefits. No strings attached. No expectations, no demands of any kind. If civilised behaviour fails, what else do we have but the primal? We can do that surely? Maul me silly, zip your pants on the porch, get into that sorry death trap you call a car and go to your child lovers. No questions, no explanations sought. It's a brutal but workable arrangement for me, unless you find me totally repulsive – which wouldn't make any sense, given that we are not strangers to each other. I know I am rambling. But that is the long and short of it ...'

Primal liaisons? I was astonished. I felt cornered. Aroused.

It dawned on me then that I did not know what to do when a woman offered herself, head bowed in modesty yet eyes ablaze with passion, a body aflame, all inhibitions discarded. Not even my ex-wife, whose body I should know, or at least claim some familiarity. What was to be done when the ways of nature were reversed, when those dictums that without saying nudge women into cocoons, where they wait, for whole lifetimes sometimes, to be seen, noticed, chosen, courted? It was not seduction, not in the purest sense, but something in between, something vague yet so evident, unwelcome but so wanted. It was something above language, above logic, something in the realm of the senses. The instinct was entrapment first, erotic second, because not all seductions are intended to end in copulation. Bed mates? What rules govern such arrangements, for is it not impossible that there could be arrangements without expectations, without someone being held accountable?

'*Ke eng, Milton, molato wa gago ke eng?*' Orapeleng droned on. '*Ga o nyake marago ka mabaka a fe?*' – What is the matter, Milton? What are your reasons for not wanting intimacies?

That is when I took my mail and walked out – into a comedy of errors. With Orapeleng following me, I had to turn back to the house to retrieve the car keys forgotten on the couch, then plead with an engine that refused to start, and when it did, discover that the rear right tyre was flat, needed changing, all the while dodging an increasingly tipsy Orapeleng determined to impose emergency love. She is very beautiful, my ex-wife, and could easily be a lost sister of the profoundly intelligent Ms Lauryn Hill – down to the full lips, and that raspy, magnetic, commanding voice.

PLEASURE

༄

I meet Orapeleng for lunch or coffee once in a while. There are loaded silences, intrusive questions, unexpected and belated compliments (she now thinks I look good in suits), cautious requests, vague admissions presented as tongue-in-cheek observations, unthinkable disclosures of expired marital venoms. She asks about Alexis, 'your Dancer Flame'. Like disabled infantrymen, we nurse our amputations, watch as nurses rinse bloody rags, wave flies off festering wounds, in the grand theatre of damaged love. And yet a mistake must not be made that Orapeleng is a warmonger. On the contrary, she can be delightful company, and is in her own way a loving woman: courteous, thoughtful, with a rare gift for acidic humour. As we sit in expensive restaurants – The Grill Club, Little Bombay, Tsunami At Sea, all popular with the chauffeur-driven types – during our post-divorce meals, those last attempts at fading romance, I am overcome by a flicker of distant grief. Not the grief of heartache or sombre things, but a lingering longing, a feeling of a precious moment lost, lost in a way that is irrevocably damaged, just as fire reduces things to soot. The divorce has not achieved anything; it was a war without spoils: no priceless paintings, no borders of conquered lands to be divided, no occupation troops to oversee, no changes of street names or false displays of goodwill, no surreptitious destruction of incriminating documents, no punitive trials to weigh and punish war crimes.

We meet at Little Bombay, scents and tastes of Calcutta held captive in Cape Town, and pontificate about the futility of matrimonial euthanasia. As Orapeleng confesses to lying awake most nights (where the fuck is her secret lover, the orthodontist, then?), I notice that the saucer is by Villeroy & Boch in New England, that the teaspoon boasts it is made of stainless steel, conclude that the violinist playing the weepy melody in low tones in the background was either a novice or lacked imagination, or may simply have been annoyed the day the recording was made. Puddles form in Orapeleng's eyes, discreet as the near-silent demise of soapsuds, but it is not her eyes that draw my attention. I finally confirm what has been an elusive discomfort for years, something that seemed improper, out of place, yet consistent with the overall picture, something that – because she was so confident about it, comfortable, not bothered by it all – blended into her being, had become *her*, and during marital feuds, was a cumbersome irritation: for a woman, Orapeleng has, at size nine, very big feet.

I miss Alexis. A few weeks before our break-up, the *Swan Lake* opening night was galloping closer and closer. Alexis had become a rare sight, except when, bruised and fatigued, she lowered herself into the front seat of the Mercedes, cupped her eyes with an open palm and drifted into immediate sleep. Overnight, she had been transformed from the darling of the dance world to a weary lover. And yet she danced away, lost herself in the sorrow of *Swan Lake*, glided feather light across the stage, twisted, bowed and turned – as if possessed, her face pained, yet graceful. My little Birdie … How could I save her from damaged pleasure intent on carving her to shreds? I nursed her bruises, bumps and collisions, kissed her skin abrasions, cooked her mutton stew on a bed of basmati rice.

And then suddenly, without warning, our romance was at sea: I battled to charm her, to keep her laughing, amused. It seemed to me that I overdid things; *fathered* her instead of loved her – for the business of being a lover is sustained by a dose of carefree moments, by caring, but not too much. My age leaped from shadows, coloured our interactions, put in question the value my years are supposed to usher in. Wisdom. Calm. Foresight. She tossed and turned in her sleep, and with determined but subdued fury commanded me to leave her alone. She was tense, even in the throes of deep sleep, wore a frown and defensive scowl. I was amazed that pleasure/love could inflict such suffering, such discomfort, such displeasure.

I learned that younger women, no matter how mature, experience life the only way nature and time demands: as *young* women. To this end, my default role was that of protective father, which was, I suppose, crude and overbearing, and not that of lover, marked by elusive sentiments. My fall was from the great pleasures of love to the average ones of listening to the sea, a leap from the grand pleasures of literary enlightenment to the mundane pleasures of scratching groins, an implosion of noble pleasures of wartime dreams to the dirty ones of clipping toenails, a nod at the universal pleasures of art to the crippled ones of addictions to coffee and the clack of the Remington's keys.

Her singular question haunts me still: 'Is it because I am not French, Milton?' But how could I convince Alexis that Marie was not French? That she may have been a real person some seventy years ago, that as far-fetched as my defence sounds, I had never met her, not in *person* anyway, and that I had not the slightest clue why I called her name in my sleep. That I had had no secret liaisons with her. That because she existed without being there, it would have been impossible, even if I had wanted to. Her forehead furrowed, her eyes narrowed, and like a hammer to the skulls she choked our union: 'I am not a child. I know about Abella Beaudrie, Milton. I saw you, followed you to Rosebank. You lied to me – said you were meeting Achille. I saw everything – you could not even keep your hands to yourself. And yet you tell me of ocean-deep love reserved only for me. I don't know you any more, Milton. Oceans are deep – that is why I believed you; because an ocean is very deep, a beautiful, powerful and mysterious thing that should hold a lot of love. Why couldn't you simply tell me, at least afford me the opportunity to make up my own mind? Tell me – please – what I have ever done to you to deserve such lies from you? Is it because I am not French?'

She broke down in a way I have never seen anyone melt, fold into themselves, and I knew ... I didn't deserve her; that it would be unjust to woo her back, which is the one and only reason I never attempted to continue being a swine. My other defence is lousy, I know, but so very true: I don't know why I do the things I do.

I spend days thinking about Orapeleng's offer – an insane offer, yes, but also a possible and not-so-unheard-of offer, one that I am sure is made all the time, that – were it not for that stupid orthodontist – could have had a slim chance of consideration.

But pleasures of *that* kind are supposed to be sacred, not contaminated by doubt or idiots in white shorts brandishing tennis racquets and lurking in the shadows. Besides, it is clear to me that my passions for her have cooled, been dealt a fatal blow. Pleasure, I have learned, is a solitary phenomenon; it does not mix well with remorse and regrets or mistakes. To be whole, be *itself*, to bloom, pleasure is unforgiving, suspicious – even in the face of the most logical and redeemable situations. It does, by its nature, overcompensate; it is premised on greed, because at its most elementary pleasure survives on selfishness, on discreet contracts, undemocratic arrangements.

Abella visits, and finds the apartment bare; it echoes.

'You like it?' I ask.

'*Oui. Beaucoup. C'est très artistique.*' – Yes. Very much. It's very arty.

'You want to spend the night?'

'With pleasure. As long as you don't touch me,' she says.

'Why would you say such a thing?' I ask, puzzled.

'*Je ne sais pas. Tu es un méchant charmeur qui caresse sans repentir. Tu ne me laisses jamais tranquille.*' – I don't know. You are a naughty, charming, unrepentant fondler. You never leave me alone.

The insinuation, the accusation, is that I am a pest intent on peering and exploring under her dress. I admit only to the act, and not necessarily its intention or her interpretation. She is both subject and accomplice, equally guilty, party to the under-dress rituals. We even had a name for it: the Storming of the Bastille.

But she is serious. She threatens to leave without so much as a peck on my cheek if I don't convincingly state what I plan to do to help my brother. My brother Bull has been arrested – the sixth time this year – for possession. Cannabis. I say I will think about it, prompting her to pace around in a huff, with an exaggerated but nevertheless real display of hurt and disappointment.

I have one of those modern, wall-mounted digital telephones with a ringtone that can be programmed: birds in a rainforest, a locomotive, or a heavy downpour. My ringtone of choice is Carlos Santana's '*Oye Como Va*', which, as I dug a little into my musical stratosphere, I learned was recorded by one Tito Puente in 1963. Abella pushes me away from the phone whenever it rings, dances to the music, including when the ringtone is set on '*Corazon Espinado*' – another Santana whirlwind that stirs Abella's dance sensibilities. But she is not dancing to Santana tonight; we have had an altercation over Alexis, over a bracelet I gifted her when she turned twenty-five – five years ago. The argument started with me lacking respect, then it was about lacking respect while expecting respect, and quickly exploded into why she was never offered a bracelet, and when all was argued and resolved, it started all over again on a very different tangent, which I concluded was the crux of the argument to start with: that Alexis, like Masechaba, was young and carefree, abundantly beautiful and therefore real and unfair competition.

She had said she was fine with what she termed my 'roving eye'. And it certainly seemed so in the first three months or so, when she would jokingly say: 'Kindergarten is out, now it's time for *real* love.' I had cautioned her against her grandstanding, to which she replied: '*Ce lit-ci est très bruyant, au fait, tes voisins doivent vraiment nous détester! Tu devrais acheter un bon lit au lieu de bracelets hors de prix!*' – This is a very noisy bed, by the way, your neighbours must really hate us! You should buy a proper bed instead of overpriced bracelets!

That was how it had all started, a fight apparently about noisy beds and overpriced bracelets, but was, in reality, a sophisticated detour to saying that she was feeling jealous and threatened by my younger lovers: *Deux Petites Souris*, the 'Two Little Mice'.

The phone rings.

'Yes?' I say after catching the handset midair when she flings it at me. 'Oh, how very nice, Achille. You sit on my manuscript for ten decades; don't even acknowledge receipt? Six weeks, ten decades, same difference! I have been waiting.'

Achille laughs.

'I am serious. You know how important this book is to me. And what do you do? You swing on my motherfucking balls, and for what?'

Achille Bemba is a dear friend, an accomplished scholar, critic, and many other things in between. He says he has read Draft Thirteen of the typescript, that he is biased but thinks 'there is something there' – his words. He warns, though, that 'Pan Africanists are going to slaughter you in the press'.

'Slaughter? For *what*?'

He laughs: 'All your French escapades and 1945 innuendos. I think the manuscript is solid, but dangerously skewed. Leopold II is, for instance, a kindred spirit of the Führer, for what he did in the Congo Free State. In fact, Leopold predates the Third Reich, because you are looking at a period 1885 to 1908. Some dramatic stuff happened, and that should make for some riveting literature.'

'How much does a soul cost, in your estimation, Achille? A dollar, forty Deutschmarks, a bag of rice? What do seventeen million souls cost? Does it matter *where* they are bought, *how* they are wasted? Of course I know about Leopold. But that is not the focus of my book. I know that no story is ever complete, Achille. And be reminded that I am not a pamphleteer – keep that in mind, you and your Pan Africanists. Leopold. Fuck!' We laugh, full of mirth, then an empty silence. I have read the history, the records. Some are already there in Draft Nine of the manuscript, all thirty pages of Leopold. It chokes you, sickens you, stifles you. Had to be culled because it just weighs down the book.

'Sections of the novel still need some serious thought and reflection. As the draft stands, you risk being branded an Uncle Tom,' Achille reiterates. He won't let it go.

'But *why*? Why is that?'

'Because. Why write selectively and indirectly about holocausts on the African continent? The near total extermination of the Herero in German West Africa is worth over a thousand books on its own. What do you have to say about that?'

'A lot. Just not in this particular book. Any other suggestions?'

Achille is firm: 'Yes. A complete rewrite.'

I find his grandstanding annoying: 'What do you think novel writing is, Achille? Pamphleteering? I write about pleasure in the same book, you know. Have you suddenly and conveniently forgotten? Aren't you supposed to be a scholar? Think, dammit!'

'I *am* thinking.'

'No, you are not. If your counter view, and that of your Pan

Africanists and nationalists for whom you have elected yourself spokesperson, is that Africans can only think and reflect on their own continent – in total isolation from world events – then you have lost your mind. I cannot accept that Africans should not dream, or imagine themselves outside of *only being black and colonised and enslaved* – as if the rest of the world is empty, and everything that happens in it has nothing to do with them whatsoever! That is demented scholarship, a very slippery ideological slope you are trying to climb. The drop down that cliff is too deep to fathom, and no nation, no people – including Africans – can survive such a drop. Such a fragmented and myopic view of history. Selective humanity. You might as well piss on your damn PhD.'

'All right, all right. Relax,' he sighs. Then says he has to go – a cheese-and-wine for some retiring academic – and promises to ring back for a longer chat.

Abella, who feigns deep sleep, is still as a gravestone. She knows I know she is being mischievous: no soul settles that quickly and permits effortless sleep when the heart poisons the mind, when a bracelet ruins all things pleasurable. I strip, walk to the Remington, sit – and listen to the rumblings of the sea.

Someone influential in Melbourne sends me a review of *Pitiful Emperors*, reflections on that beloved novel that almost put me on the same pedestal as Father. It is the only one of my eleven books that Father read at least thrice, never once in my presence. I tiptoed into his study one winter, during one of my rare visits to Casablanca Estates when I burdened him with my marital poisons, he in dreamland by way of an afternoon siesta, and found he had three copies of all *Pitiful Emperors* editions, all of which had page markers, underlining in different coloured pens, pages that had modest water damage: drinking water, whisky, tears? There is, in the *New Thinker Review of Books*, continued futile comparisons laced with caveats: is the son as good as the father (he is supremely gifted), will he ever be comparable to the father (in certain instances), will he ever beat the father (with years of work, but even then, possible but unlikely)? I could sense that Father loved *Pitiful Emperors*, though he never once said a word about it. Not once. I imagine it gave him great pleasure knowing I knew all that I explored in the book: why else would he underline so many paragraphs in three different editions? And yet there remained a void: seemingly timeless, artistically urgent, without witnesses or form. It was this predicament, of wanting to impose form onto the void, that I began selling off father's furniture – everything, including that noisy bed – to rid the apartment of him, to leave a sure echo of me: my footsteps, my thoughts, sneezes, of the sea, most of all the sea. Only the burgundy curtains remain, them and the Remington. I have procured a futon bed, comfortable and silent, even with the most restless sleep.

Abella visited last Thursday, said: '*Les lits sont des déclarations de plaisir en soi, n'est-ce pas? Imagine s'il n'y avait pas un seul lit dans l'univers: pas de rêves, pas de larmes intimes dans les oreillers, pas de susurrements des mots doux à l'oreille des amants, pas de moments passés à regarder vaguement le plafond et imaginer ... Moi, je mérite tous les plaisirs de la vie.*' – Beds are pleasure statements in themselves, no? Imagine if there wasn't a single bed in the universe: no dreams, no private weeping into pillows, no whispering things into the ears of lovers, no staring at the ceiling and imagining ... I deserve all of life's pleasures.

All of life's pleasures. Imagine that!

Hooded and in track pants, I use the back door down a poorly lit staircase, and onto the street where I mingle with the living: those under no yokes or spells to author masterpieces. The lie remains on the front door – misinformation: that I am in Johannesburg. I know Abella has looked for me, tried to track me down at our hangout spots around Cape Town, in coffee shops, movie theatres, countless times at Apartment 4003, her voice cancelling all others on the answering machine, in the post, on Table Mountain walking trails, the Franschhoek winelands – more blind fumbling than any real hope she would find me.

It is not out of discourtesy that I act as I do, not out of any vengeance or ill feelings, but rather my search, compulsion, the urge to do justice to all the horrors in what could have been Marie's photographs: my God, look at this one, the furnace, the chimneys, this heap of ash. *Gerechtigkeit!* Just treatment for every confused child, dusty and hungry and thirsty and cold, scolded in hisses under wooden floors and in attics by paranoid parents, who had no words and time and safe places to explain why they had to wear the Star of David armbands. *Spravedlnost!* for every boy or girl, hushed and starved and cuddled until the last of the SS left, following floor, ceiling and wardrobe searches via machine-gun fire, a generation of mute and lonesome mouths bloomed:

children who because they were children, without an immediate understanding of death, of self-preservation, whose natural state was horsing around and falling asleep with shoes still on, or neck twisted under a table and a doll still in hand, drooling creatures to be carried to bed and hugged and kissed and tucked in, shoes removed, and allowed to slumber in comfort. *Ikpe ziri ezi!* for those searches, with their accompanying yells and by gunfire, often punctured pillows, sending feathers flying, or shattered mirrors that crashed like avalanches, but also warm blood from hiding children who had drifted off to sleep behind wardrobe doors, who died without knowing they were dying, whom bullets tore to shreds with deadly indifference. *Justicia*, for children who looked up to once respected rabbis and uncles, fathers and aunts, shoved, searched, yelled at and spat upon. Wide-eyed their faces sought answers, only to be met by stony and forbidding faces of humiliated uncles, grateful and anxious and infuriated still to be alive. *Whakawa!* for children who would hide in latrines and cowsheds and open fields, under bathtubs and under giant flowerpots, children scattered and cold in cemeteries: hunted, captured, herded onto Eichmann's trains. Maybe there was perverse pleasure in that, in hunting children like one hunts rabbits or squirrels; maybe there was some benefit to the soul, too complex to be untangled: all those children loaded into trains, trampled and squeezed and dozing, unaware of their unawareness that something unpleasant was unfolding. But *unpleasant* is the wrong word; it implies a simple irritation, a temporary discomfort of a cerebral and emotional nature, does nothing to illuminate the true measure of the extreme of that unpleasantness. It is a placeholder word, misleading, used only while a more

PLEASURE

appropriate word, with adequate weight, directness, is searched. A word stripped of all pretensions: *evil*.

I am learning, rather late at fifty-six, that for all our misconceptions, our old-age truths, nothing – absolutely nothing – compares to the glow of pleasure, which, like snowflakes, blankets the world in mock coldness, in temporary chills meant to hide, to distort, to obscure the true heat lurking in every flake. That pleasure is not something one studies, categorises or explains, something one possesses or saves and shows off; those snowflakes can form and melt away in front of your very eyes: patient, silent, pure. Flakes that induce fevers – some grand, some laughable – fevers called infatuation, desire. Even love. To steal even a glance at pleasure – that ethereal snowflake – from the safety of ignorance, I learn, those Remington keys in full flight, that one cannot afford clutter, distractions of whatever kind. Pleasure, the Remington and I record, is not a feeling one *seeks*, but one that just *is*. Like the waters of the sea seen from behind these hideous curtains, pleasure is indifferent to its own power, its beauty, its destructiveness. I further learn that one is measured by pleasure, is marked, chosen, cajoled, then possibly crushed. That not even a trillion Remingtons, ringing their bells day and night, are equal to the magnitude of pleasures' deceptions, its matter-of-factness. Ask Philip Roth. Even he, the master, has barely scratched the surface. And as you might know, Roth at his best writes crystal-clear prose – sentences and phrases that sing, images you can almost taste.

But I digress ...

The manuscript is cooking me alive – from the inside out, a burn that is aloof but there, slow, leaving not a grain of ash. It is possible that it will never be written, not to completion. One cannot rely on the world of dreams – cannot ask Marie to interpret her midnight baths, to rebel against her housekeeping chores. Even if I had invited her to bed, assuming she would have agreed, all nude and supple, nothing could be done because she was there without being there; her being there was a mirage, a false picture, false emotion, false possibilities. Even the averting of my gaze was a sham, hollow cowardice, mock shame – not shame in its gnawing sense, known to shrink and immobilise, but mock shame: because even in the throes of sleep, tossing and turning in that noisy bed, Alexis' palm resting on my lower back, there lurked in my desire, in my basking in mock pleasure, in my liaisons with Marie, real and felt lust that dissipated the moment I woke, only to be replaced by insistent longing for a flesh-and-blood Alexis in my bed, the one sound asleep beside me.

Is the suffering that is endured in dreams *real* suffering, or a mind engaged with the business of living? People dream: friends, lovers, dictators. Are we then to seek life's answers in passive states, where we can kiss and jump off cliffs and pilot planes and trade in diamonds and wake up to find we have been duped, mocked and betrayed even? As far as entertainment goes, my dreams surpass even the most accomplished of motion pictures; so rich and layered, so pleasurable and terrifying that they occupy me for weeks on end. I am tempted to wallow in them, to ask questions, yearn to have relations with strangers in them. It disturbs me when a dream finishes mid-action, leaving me to wonder and imagine what the outcome would have been, whether it could be paused for closer observation.

All Achille's cautions about Pan Africanists find only distant resonance with me – but the Marie Dream consumes me. We – Achille and I – speak about the manuscript, telephonic discussions that elope into sleepy mumbling in the early hours: what we perceive to be the climax of the novel, how the Marie Dream possibly holds the novel to ransom, dares me to touch it, without ruining the story, and how passive lusts may annoy some adventurous readers.

'Let's face it,' charges Achille, 'some readers relish blood and gore, detest half steps, want things as they are: crude and raw. You cannot be a gentleman and a writer at the same time. Choose a cause. When are you going to live, walk on the edge? Would you sleep a wink if you lived a little, or would your conscience chew you to shreds? How do you even call yourself a writer if you taste life by the fingernail? Don't you know real artists live, and only then create? How do you expect to be like your father? That man – and I mean no disrespect – was sleek, measured, but I am not sorry he is dead. I doubt there is a forbidden fruit he has not sampled, your father. Ask me. I know. I saw him, bumped into him in places, met him in compromising circumstances. He laughed everything off, dismissed whatever indiscretion, however grave, with a casual nod. You have shackled yourself, holed up in an apartment writing a masterpiece? Who cares? You think anyone knows you live such a bland, sanitised, uneventful life? Why don't you just walk to the sea and drown yourself? Because you're long dead anyway … Come now, man!' He is out of breath – speaking too passionately. 'And live a little! What could possibly be sadder than a fifty-six-year-old holed up behind your hideous curtains?'

He is not aware how depressed I have been, how loneliness has snuffed the life out of me, how I live in the dark, how the apartment is strewn with books and papers of all kinds, how I survive on apples and water. I soak in the bath, soak and cry, and in that wounded state I answer him: 'Readers? It's my book! So what if they hate it?'

Achille cautions that I am getting carried away, shooting the messenger, and reminds me: 'It is just a book. Relax.'

'You are wrong. It is *not* just a book,' I tell him. 'People died there. *Human beings*. Why wouldn't anyone want to acknowledge, understand that?' I hang up – more, I think, because of the unpalatable things he has been saying about Alexis lately, things that annoy me about him.

Bull, my younger brother, called. I am not entirely sure what made me answer that particular call, and still disregard all the others, but I picked up. Bull said he had been giving serious thought to killing himself and wanted to know what *I* thought about that. I just sat there perspiring, butt naked, with the receiver pressed against my ear. He ranted about why police never tired of arresting him, opined that there are far greater and unacceptable crimes than cannabis usage. That a charge for possession is draconian as there is no way of proving without a shadow of a doubt that there was intended use.

'What if I intended quitting?' he asked. 'How would the arresting officer possibly *know* that?' There was a long pause, just breathing, after which Bull confessed that he owed money to some really bad people who have sworn on their grandmothers' graves to kill him; that he thought it may be dignified to beat them to it.

So, what did he do? He overdosed on laxatives, that's what. Ran in and out of the bathroom for three days and nights, and was finally admitted for dehydration and inflammation of the stomach lining. Wrist slitting seemed too dramatic, it seemed, lacking in imagination, too overused, prompting him to then attempt to gas himself with exhaust fumes from his clapped-out old Datsun – only it had no fuel, so the engine wouldn't start. So, frustrated, he telephoned the ringleader of bad men he owed and threatened to chew his testicles raw. Realising he had just worsened the situation, he continued on his quest of self-destruction, resorted to a foolproof plan that saw him prostrating himself on the Park Station railway tracks – only to be told two hours later by amused passers-by that the train drivers were on an indefinite strike. He just sat there, sunburned and exhausted, lit a joint and puffed his way past plainclothes police officers, who casually dangled handcuffs in his face.

Since Bull's inheritance ran out, since he ran down the petrol-station business, the family lawyer has stopped taking his calls, started shouting profanities at him – one of which, says Bull, chuckling mirthfully, has Rudolph calling him a 'weed-smoking goat stuck in the sewers of self-pity and denial'. That lawyer has a way with words, should have been a writer, I told Bull.

'Writers,' he answered, 'are thieves of people's time, their emotions, their perceptions of the world, their lives. They are enforcers, varied in their madness. The essence of writing is spending a lifetime behind typewriters, computers, making up things – a lazy way of earning a living – while people with a true passion for work toil in fields in the blazing sun, harvest food in incontinent weather, lay railway lines across vast landscapes, keep the clientele of whorehouses entertained.' There was a pause, as though his mind, his thoughts, were trying to catch up with his mouth, his words. 'But don't get me wrong ... I value literature, men and women of letters; minds, great and small, recording, twisting, deforming, and illuminating life – and yet, and yet, no great book has answers to the perils of existence. None. They are all attempts, all false starts. What have they changed?'

I never imagined cannabis would trigger such a rousing, impassioned speech, a speech that almost left me in tears – tears because of how my brother treats me. A speech, flawed in content, but almost convincing in its philosophical premise: that nothing, not even great books, make the slightest dent against existence.

He wanted bail money, of course – so desperately, in fact, that he threatened to jump in front of the very first train he came across upon release, a tragedy that could be readily avoided if I promptly paid the money. I gently placed the receiver on the phone, thus ending the call. Please understand: my brother has been threatening to kill himself ever since we were seven, and frankly, I couldn't care less if a cat scratched him to death, if he choked on cannabis seeds, if errant gangsters cracked his skull with a baseball bat. I know my brother too well, and I can say without hesitation that everything he says is a figment of his imagination. He will be alive – albeit stoned – for many decades to come.

Who is to say that Giovanni Gomez derived no pleasure from Elisabeth's fleshy underarms? What if those armpits, sweaty and sticky, were to him keys to boundless bliss? Who is to say – more fundamentally – that the Elizabeths of the world belong only to beds at twilight, that their plump thighs bolt them to their husbands, that they have no lives of their own, that they have neither drive nor passion to convene and direct Nurembergs? Can it be concluded, with any measure of certainty, that Giovanni's Elisabeth does not lie in bed, pondering the cards she holds, cards with which to rewrite the protocols of war? To, instead of declaring war, clean cemeteries, use war purses to pay poets, rid the world of noisy beds? Surely Elisabeth has views on pleasure; possibly insightful ones, outrageous ones, views that would have heated and congealed, gathered dust and died because Giovanni was away from home, relishing murdering Germans.

How is it that I – even with Abella, my most vocal of lovers – fail to trace pleasure contours of women I love? Is this the price one pays for being a sloppy womaniser: this blindness, detachment, this ignorance when it comes to cathedrals of pleasure? Who, in peace times and in war, determines who is considered a competent womaniser? Do womanisers, except for the ruthlessness as alleged by Orapeleng, have specific composure, particular sensibilities, language tailored to sustain their craft? And how does one transform all these into fiery literature?

I – though it would be hard to prove, impossible even – submit that a certain radiance enters a man who thinks and writes in the nude. Hard as Father's chair is and, the Remington keys stingy and unyielding, and those burgundy curtains hiding and revealing the sea, I continue to exist among Capetonians. I observe them, oblivious to the nudist who slaves, with back upright, in front of the Remington. I see them kiss pregnant wives at Little Bombay, see their umbrellas collide on narrow sidewalks, how they sacrifice newspapers to sudden downpours. I sit behind the slightly drawn curtains, cigarette in one hand and wine glass in another, and watch the sea: when it is a bluish silver from the midday sun, when it turns gold from the afternoon sun, its transition into a grey morass with foamy waves come early evening, and a black giant plotting in the dark come nightfall. I watch helicopter searchlights momentarily undress the sea, peep into its secrets, accuse it of stealing and hiding things: drunks, the suicidal, battered boats drifting off course.

The street below is obviously *in* Cape Town, but it could be a street anywhere in the world: Madrid, for instance, on the French Riviera, in Nairobi, even Lower Manhattan. How petty, the differences, those variations in geography; how little or no difference they make in the *essence* of pleasure. It dawns on me that Cape Town, with all its beauty and charms, its prime spots, remains but a transit stop for pleasure – that the Remington would continue ringing to eternity if I don't free myself from my nude toils, because location – whether Rio de Janeiro or Maputo, Algiers or Dortmund – matters not in the realm of pleasure. The constant is that most will seek it, have it imposed on them, deny themselves its flames, abuse it and in turn be obliterated by it.

Even when denied, curtailed, policed, even when suppressed, pleasure – like the truth, defiant in Marie's photographs – insists on rearing its head, on its own terms. Neither Achille nor his Pan Africanists can contain either pleasure or truth, for what ideology has ever been greater than sensation, than the dictates of conscience? Even hardened Sorbibor or Treblinka guards had wives, daughters upon whom they wished good fortune, delightful lives filled with pleasures. Then and now, pleasure predates everything. The beginning of a life finds it *already* in full swing, and an ending of one or thirty-four million makes not even the slightest dent against it. And so they lied, the swine, fearful of being hanged, of firing squads marching them to walls, feigning insanity to deny complicity because of a paramount fear that when that hangman's noose gripped the neck, when firing squads squinted one eye and took aim, when cyanide was the only option, life's pleasures would cease.

Think about that for a moment: total erasure, leaving behind scorned corpses and despised names. Even when herded like cattle into Eichmann's trains, pleasure never left. She was there: as warmth, in the nervous twitching smiles of merciful guards with conflicted consciences, in sunsets, in the relief of being enslaved rather than culled, in flowers across open plains. A wave of shame washes over me. How dare I write such grave matters in the nude? Can it be argued that nudity is the ultimate respect, the profoundest and most primal of states?

Photographers will, for centuries to come, point lenses at wild flowers blooming in fiery reds and inviting yellows, adorning hillsides and open fields. Young boys will pick one or two blossoms and, with some nervous poetry recitals, warm the hearts of girls on picnics, embalm them with pleasure without bounds. Those flowers, wild and carefree, radiant and inviting, will, for those in the know, never quite be beautiful. Sure, they will deceive, flutter in the breeze, enthral butterflies. But they will, for those in the know, remain of cursed beauty, meaningless charm. It would be better if there are only boulders, rough and lifeless things, as opposed to such luminance of flowers that adorn the hills, atop mass graves, their beauty parasitic, fed by countless truckloads laden with those whom furnaces could not consume. Historians, archaeologists and mining prospectors will one day discover new fragments, the remains of what used to be someone's jacket, blackened, rotten and shredded, the Star of David eaten by an indifferent earth. As seasons change, as flowers wither into worthless tinder prone to veld fires, as bees lose interest and butterflies disappear, as the countryside deadens, the bones will lie awake, in protest and decay. Protest at the manner and scale of their obliteration. Accusatory questions will remain, challenging those flowers: how dare you bloom, what right have you, have you no shame waltzing in the breeze when what lies beneath the very ground on which you stand are wrist bones still clutching rosaries, a dental crown on a skull (how did they miss that one?), rusty jacket buttons that just won't turn to dust?

I don't think of myself as an unskilled lover – in fact, not at all. Why these three women, excluding my former wife, graced my bed have to do with matters I would rather not discuss – except to present as cold facts and observations that have so enthralled me, so elated me, so transformed me that I would have been insane not to surrender: Alexis' varied smiles, Abella's liveliness on the tennis court, the abundance of her strength, and Masechaba's mouth, those lips with their curves and twitchy ways, her boundless empathy and adoration of children, are facets not easily found in a single jewel. Oh, to see Alexis smile, watch her glide on the dance floor, her feet barely touching the ground. Or be amused by a tipsy Masechaba, hear her speak about faraway planets, wonder if there is water on Mars. How could anyone possibly not love all three – not necessarily in equal measure, but enough to dim the stars?

My reluctance to fight for my lovers, to charm them, to grovel and win them back, has to do with the fact that I find it difficult, if not impossible to accept that these fine women – the finest in my eyes – exist for the sole purpose of my vanity. Ugly as it may sound, when all else is disregarded, I have concluded that: one, I allowed my marriage to perish; two, life is short so I might as well have some fun; three, one knows little or nothing about women even at age fifty-six; and finally, four, there is a difference between being in *love* and *connecting*. How profound. Who knew?

My self-imposed seclusion has little or nothing to do with being a solitary creature. Part of it is that an overwhelming sense of shame gnaws at me – even when I am at my happiest. There must have been a better way, a way that demanded more effort on my part, a clearer sharing of feelings when it came to my three lovers. I don't think cowardice explains anything, that it is even part of the equation, but my aversion to the phone and those knocks on the door are at least a belated acknowledgement, a realisation that I have been a tacky lover. I have, on the brink of tears, lips trembling, said as much to all three of my beloveds – a confession casually dismissed as 'a performance'. Without even realising it, I adopted Alexis' mathematical sensibilities, imagined the measuring and weighing of everything: looking at an aircraft flying overhead and estimating its dimensions, or the singular and combined weight of femurs on an athlete breaking records at the Olympic Games, the weight in grams of twelve thousand snowflakes. From Masechaba I learned how to insert and extract myself from arguments, practise diplomacy, to be everything to everyone without losing integrity or abandoning my beliefs; and my acute sense of empathy, a fascination with the Storming of the Bastille, with history as real lives and events past, would never have flourished had it not been for Abella Beaudrie. I recall snippets of conversations with all three of my beloveds that touched, for example, on the Manhattan Project and the French Revolution (Abella), on estimated distances travelled by lovers' hearts in millimetres and split seconds during lovers' doubts or hurt (Alexis), and with Masechaba the complete overhaul of arguments for their own sake – that is, to ensure an end to petty squabbles and reckless talk, the promulgation of an international law that criminalises weak and vindictive arguments without overwhelming proof in professional and personal life, punishable by twelve months of silence, the violation of that imposed silence multiplying the year of imprisonment by three. In her words, this meant the 'birthing of distilled thought through responsible arguments' worthy of humans as an apex species. But Orapeleng is reckless in her conclusions, branding me a hopeless womaniser and a coward – offending me, and by implication, insulting my beloveds as empty vessels: born for the sole purpose of being pleasure pots, without further thought or purpose.

What would Orapeleng make of this not opening of doors, the phone left to ring, unattended? Would she still think it weakness, a lack of skill, cowardice perhaps? Cowardice: an accusation that paralyses me in many ways because the sphere of that cowardice was never disclosed. Was it, for example, a fear of dying, of the dark, of women? Was it perhaps an aversion to failure or illness, or simply failure to confront that which brought me displeasure? Is this what Alexis meant when she suggested, all tearful and morose – which was unlike her – that there remained, even at my most passionate, my most involved during our most heartfelt encounters, a fading light at the very centre of my soul? That there was always a lack, a yearning, a search that disregarded the fact that *she* was there, giving her all, her admirable knickers coiled on her left ankle, in an act of simultaneous passion and sacrifice. It is not sex you want, Alexis cautioned, but something far greater and much more precarious, something I cannot begin to imagine, let alone name.

The void I imagined I kept to myself began swallowing up every aspect of my existence: my teaching, my brother Bull, my three loves, the apartment, the Remington, even the sea beyond those curtains. The writing of this manuscript, with all its false sparks, its contortions and murky swamps, seems to be all I have, a brittle pillar supporting my termite-eaten soul, a soul threatening to collapse in one dusty, cobweb-ridden mess. Whatever does or doesn't happen, there remains in me a faint voice, barely audible, a child's voice, a playful voice that without emotion or dictation, without urgency or grandeur, without even the slightest hint of expectation, says: 'There is truth in dreams.'

The phone stops ringing, the knocks on the door fade away, leaving only echoes of my own footsteps around the apartment, a nude chain-smoker drowning in wine and the indifferent rumble of the sea. But with that comes the realisation that what I long concluded to be an approaching ending, at least a near-fatal blow, to my life and that of the manuscript, seems instead to be the sound of enlightenment approaching, crawling nearer, from a billion light years away. Enlightenment. Lucidity. Suffering.

There lies, beyond the comforts of Casablanca Estates, around the outskirts of this metropolis – away from its wealth, beauty and snobbery – another world: a world inhibited by black faces, other faces. It is these faces the city sucks into its web, to shine its bank floors and prune its hedges, to scrub algae from its swimming pools, attend to its cash registers come morning; faces the city will chew, spit and expel come evening. To Langa the faces will return, to Bonteheuwel and Gugulethu and Mitchell's Plain, to join black and other faces that cannot get away to the trappings of Clifton and Casablanca Estates, to escape a grinding lack of almost everything: food, hope, dignity. Homes. From the worst food high blood pressures peak, from self-styled James Bonds bodies fall, from despair lifetimes leak away, leaving scrawny, trigger-happy and temperamental youths lurking at street corners. And yet there are, among the faceless faces, strained and voiceless, little miracles: of the young and daring refusing to be swallowed by history, who with candle light illuminate theories of Pythagoras, who skin rats and frogs to one day perform triple heart bypasses, who stare at starry nights to calm raging hearts. In the grand castles of Bishopscourt and Constantia they slave – yearn and dream and imagine life's pleasures they might never have, trapped by known but ignored webs: setting Camps Bay dinner tables, mowing Clifton lawns, and walking Fresnaye dogs; dogs with better menus and medical insurance than them.

It is the most peculiar arrangement, this courting and dismissal of faces, much like one chews and then discards gum. Not Sorbibor, not quite; not Treblinka – strictly speaking – for there are no guards in lookout towers, no ash falling from gloomy skies, but still lifetimes of strife, of heartache, of obscurity. The president says things are changing. That might or might not be true. It is also possible that the ghettos, those conveyor belts of misery – mostly peopled by Africans, who so badly and rightly want things to change – have started believing in shadows, in imaginary but attainable Edens.

My Marie Dream, the backbone of my manuscript, is flawed. Fatally so. Specifically, Giovanni's life as it relates to mine, and the dangerous licence the dream takes with historical and chronological time. The attempt to assassinate the Führer at the *Wolfschanze*, my research tells me, took place between 1943 and 1944 (there would be some three or more attempts), but the dream would have me believe that it was a single attempt in 1945; that Field Marshal Rommel's North Africa campaign, Powell's Stalingrad misadventures (1942–43) occurred within months, when in reality, events unfolded over a year. It is also very unlikely that Giovanni Gomez would have, as a prisoner of war, enjoyed such lavish perks – let alone Marie's nocturnal escapades – if the Manhattan Project was indeed the reason for his imprisonment. Was it even possible, thinkable, that the Führer would have risked the reputation of the Reich on Marie, a young and traumatised photographer, hopping from camp to camp, photographing things? Would Eichmann or Goebbels have placed stacks of photographs in front of the Führer, said: *'Alles in ordnung, mein Führer. Wir machen gute Fortschritte'* – All is well, my Führer. We are making great progress? They would have surely detected weakness, a conflicted conscience in Marie, an empathy not consistent with the gallant march of the Reich set to last for a thousand years! Shot her in the head. It was also, on closer inspection, according to documentary photographs, inaccurate that SS boots had bootlaces, for they were knee-high things in supple leather, smooth and calf hugging. It would have, therefore, been impossible for Giovanni to decode SS personalities based on individual soldiers' relationships with bootlaces!

But it is not completely useless, my dream, for there is overwhelming evidence that persons and events in it closely resemble those of 1930 to 1945 Germany. The jury is still out on whether Giovanni Gomez ever existed, whether as an individual or his variations, a composite character. And yet he existed enough to grace my dream in such detail and clarity as to make it impossible for me ignore him. That walk of his through my dream and therefore my life was calculated, thought through, not without foreplanning, choice omissions. There wasn't, for instance, long as that dream was, a single sighting of a sign that said: '*Juden, Achtung! Der weg nach Palästina führt nicht durch diesen ort!*' – We don't want to see Jews. They are our problem, or The Road to Palestine is not through here. Not even a lone Star of David on the sidewalk. Nothing untoward: except for that ash.

It turns out I am more like Giovanni Gomez than I thought. I sit in front of the Remington and sob; I do not have the courage to even lift my fingers to the keys. I feel empty, numb, and cannot master any form of composure. My brother, my brother, my father's child, I weep and bang my fists on the table in rage and despair. My book killed my brother, drove him to the train tracks, newspapers describing the goriest scenes: of bone fragments and other unmentionables. The weight of it, how it snuffs out any possibility of self-control, that bottomless grief dressed in guilt has turned me into a nauseous nudist whose stomach holds nothing down. My sprints to the toilet bowl are frequent – even when there is nothing to vomit, just suppressed wails and spitting, the bellows of an animal being slaughtered. I eat nothing, drink nothing, sit shivering behind the burgundy curtains looking at the sea by day and listening to it by night. I am gripped by a fever the likes of which I have never known – not a sickness, with which fevers are associated, but an inability to feel, to take in my surroundings. The sea. All I have is the sea, murmuring in the night, breaking small waves, moderate ones, towering mountains of water rising and falling in a magnetic buzz. He meant it, I mutter to myself, he meant it; he reached out to me and I let him down. How was I to know, with that playfulness in his voice, a twinkle in his eyes I knew to be his trademark, that he was serious: a voice he had used to worry, blackmail and con me for decades, used to distort and exaggerate all sorts of dangers, invent problems, misrepresent facts, corner me into far-fetched but plausible scenarios that without fail cost me money, and when all failed, to evoke silence that could last for months until I, out of guilt, would pick up the phone to trace his whereabouts. I would be met with a flurry of news, his tone not in the least affected by the circumstances of our parting, the lapse in time, or remorse of the faintest hue: 'I think Miranda is pregnant. Again! I don't know what I am going to do. She is crazy, man. Crazy.' Or 'Doctors say I have cancer. No, wait, not *cancer* cancer, but something very close to it. I need some money to check if it is indeed *cancer* cancer or a misdiagnosis.' Or 'That cancer story turned out to not be cancer. But I have a lump on my crotch that has doctors worried!' I would wait an hour or two, telephone his long-time lover, Bessie, who, amused, would say: 'Cancer? What lump? The only lump is him! His only real problem is that he is broke, and owes money to a bunch of dangerous people. He's fit as a royal horse!'

I curl up on the floor. Sob. Weep.

The sun rises, sets, plays hide and seek from behind the clouds over the sea. So does my heart, a heart that now skips beats.

I cannot accept the callousness of Bull's passing, the void into which it has plunged me. I have easy tears, continue sitting in the nude, staring vacantly at the horizon, over and beyond the sea. I have not written a word in weeks, and fear I might never again manage a single word, a feeble thought, a grain of emotion as long as railway lines exist. The apartment echoes my sobs back to me; my vision is at times blurry, so hazy that sometimes – were it not for its constant murmurs – I think the sea has evaporated. There won't be a funeral; maybe a memorial service of a very private kind, witnessed by the symphonies of the sea. The receiver shook in my trembling hand: 'Not dismembered,' announced the pathologist at the crime scene, 'not even shredded, more like *obliterated*. There was nothing to photograph, let alone recover – so long and so frequent were the trains.'

Someone – probably someone famous, a member of a band or a solitary egotist perhaps – practises electric guitar somewhere in the east wing of Casablanca Estates. Night calm picks sounds from wherever he strums his instrument, tosses them across a nearby room, blanketing us with string music: famous Jimi Hendrix licks, some laid-back ballads. I resist the urge to embarrass myself, to ignite a friendship that will last a thousand years, by following the sound, tracking it by ear to its source, knocking at the door, stretching out my hand and saying: 'Hello. My name is Milton. You play beautifully.' But I have learned that not all pleasures should be scrutinised, fully known, owned. I know that whoever strums 'Sweet Child O' Mine' solos past midnight has no clue there is a nudist slaving alongside him on a Remington. So pleasurable are the guitar sessions, so beautifully played, that neighbours have not once complained about noise or disturbance of the peace. Maybe the guitarist knows we have no choice but eat out of his palm as he turns Casablanca Estates into a rehearsal studio for famous recordings. It is this pleasure, the pleasure of the unknown guitarist that puts a spring in my step, that momentarily calms my erratic thoughts, my plundered heart. Whistling the guitarist's melodies, including pauses and polished endings, I walk downstairs, again through the back door and through the underground parking, away from preying eyes, and walk eight blocks south, where I occasionally help out at a soup kitchen for homeless Capetonians.

It never fails to disturb me to watch as the greasy and beholden on grime crawl out of their burrows, dragging dirty blankets and mysterious possessions (a rusty bicycle wheel, empty perfume bottle, orphaned red stiletto) for soup and two slices of bread. Most are pleased to see me, welcome me with open arms, take me into their sticky embraces, press me to their filthy clothes, their pungent clothes, their warm bosoms. What stops me from offering free baths at Apartment 4003 Casablanca Estates? What cautions me against insisting on and enforcing a bathers' line until the last of the grimy bodies is scrubbed, fed, made whole? Is there any pleasure at all in eating, while nursing weeks', months', even years' worth of sweat, of smells? Maybe. Maybe not. And yet there is indeed pleasure in seeing them pounce on their soup, transformed from morose introverts to talkative voyeurs, would-be friends, givers of advice, faces the metropolis has chewed but cannot spit out, souls seemingly without desires, who have in their own particular ways given up on life, on being respectable citizens, who have, in their own obscure ways, become deaf to mutters accusing them of being dirty and smelly.

I feel drawn to their wasted lives – dirty and incoherent; pulled in a way I cannot explain. Even my most inspired literary explorations seem stillborn, off key, lacking in the eloquence demanded by their suffering. It is like trying to set fire to boulders, insolent things that refuse to combust. What remains is a feeling of defeat, of surrender to an indifferent enemy, a brutal enemy not concerned with or bothered by victory or defeat. Day and night the Remington keys thunder, yielding nothing by way of literary illumination – not even a shadow of a shadow – while they continue dragging their dirty blankets, eating with both hands, belching like scoundrels.

True intercourse of the body is impossible, worthless, if not accompanied by that of the *mind*. Ours, Abella's and mine, our intercourse of the mind explored anything from revolutions to social outrage, and in that uncomfortable bed imagined and recast life and time, discussions and musings that occupied us well past midnight. There were days and nights when we delayed, completely forgot or completely disregarded intercourse of the body because our mind connections were themselves so pleasurable, so unexpected, so rewarding.

'What if the Führer was never born?' asked Abella. 'And if he was born, what if he was never in the military? What would have become of him if he became a great and celebrated painter – a Gerard Sekoto or Modigliani? Would things have been different if the Allies stood against Uncle Joe, if they punished him for the Gulags, if Germany remained peaceful and prosperous and loved?' It was and is interesting, said Abella, that 'the same 1793 *outrage* that condemned Louis XVI and Marie Antoinette to the guillotine was the very same *compassion* that drove French families to risk it all, to – aware of and fully appraised of consequences of dissent – hide children fleeing Eichmann's trains. That, in turn, must have bestowed on the children living their lives in attics and cowsheds, in the shadows, a great measure of worthless worthiness, of bottomless and conflicted gratitude directed not at individual Babineauxes, Lévesques and Rousseaus for preserving their lives, but at the boundless capacity of humanity to self-correct.'

That being so, I told her, means that the natural state of humanity should not be one of strife but of pleasure, of calm, romance, death as scheduled by God and not the Führer (and other despots), of the preservation of innocence at all costs.

Abella Beaudrie told me countless stories of her childhood: sad ones, hilarious ones, silly ones; how, for instance, she thought baby prams came equipped with real babies. I laughed so hard. I told her that you would, for that scenario to work, need a copulation factory, couples and strangers whose life mission would be to copulate, complete with doctors and midwives and designers to match each baby to a pram. And that that would mean two conveyor belts – one for prams and another for babies – meeting at an assembly point where babies get placed in prams with nannies already on standby. Both baby and pram would then be loaded onto trucks, to ships and planes for deliveries to stores around the world. Prams with faulty wheels would be returned; ugly babies shunned, proof of purchase required and better-looking babies demanded. A human factory: matrimonial pleasures and squabbles would fly out the window, to be replaced by credit-card transactions. We laughed deep into the night, serenaded by the enigmatic guitarist strumming Bob Dylan, but without the vocals and harmonica. She laughed with such force of life, Professor Beaudrie, such intensity that tears streamed down her cheeks, prompting her to sprint to the bathroom and, through the slightly open door, chuckle: *'Je dois faire pipi. Imagine des bébés vivants sur des tapis roulants – gonflés de lait et pesés. Dingue. De la pure folie.'* – I have to pee. Imagine live babies on conveyor belts – pumped full of milk and weighed. Crazy. Pure madness.

A block or so from Little Bombay, to the west, is the Florentino Ariza florist, the biggest of its kind, trading in all sorts of flowers: birthday bouquets, lone red roses for teenage lovers, wreaths for the grief stricken, potted seedlings, gala-dinner arrangements. The shop has Father's mind and heart prints everywhere: the ceramic flower stalls, the over-sized paintings, the low-hanging chandeliers, the adjacent Milton Coffees, both shops my inheritance. I make a hundred times more money selling flowers than selling books.

Maxwell – Maxwell Coetzee – manages the flower shop, grins at our clients, and steals from me in between. I know. He knows that I know, and yet continues to pilfer profits, service never-ending debts. He is a firm hand, a better manager than I will ever be, so much so that he, in a way, *deserves* more money. He deserves as much for thinking out of the box: those alliances he has built with funeral homes, party and wedding planners, love-themed stores and event organisers have brought in so much money that I am now in a position to re-evaluate my relationship with the Culture Institute. I am going to fire him one day, maybe soon, though I don't know when exactly. Not because he is incompetent or a thief, but because he believes he is *entitled* to things. That he is, in some strange way, entitled to my inheritance. I see it in his eyes that he does not want me at the Florentino Ariza, that he is happiest only when I come to collect money for banking – something that has to change, given the amounts involved.

Maxwell is hopeless at managing risk, is not at all imaginative. He thinks no one is watching or interested in the fact that the shop is so popular, so profitable. I instruct him to engage a professional cash transit company. He grudgingly agrees, but drags his feet. There is now an auditor on site – installed by me without consulting him – and suddenly profits are up some thirty per cent. Maxwell wallows in shame, is morose, edgy, temperamental. He has bought himself a brand-new BMW – the same man who, before his interview with Father, had a less-than-impressive pair of shoes. Someone says he has also bought himself property on a golf estate, that he has a Jacuzzi to fit ten Sumo wrestlers where he entertains, some say, under-aged girls.

PLEASURE

Short, sturdy, and on the plump side, Maxwell is not what you would call a shameless, greedy thief – simply because he *knows* what he is doing *is* wrong. It shames him, makes his eyes dart all over and, at worst, forces him to call in sick, again pushing profits to climb a further ten per cent.

How does he get past you, I ask Frik de Waal, the auditor, to which Frik answers: '*Fokken vark; ek weet nie. Hy's klaar vrot.*' – Fucking swine; I don't know. He's rotten to the core.

But I insist we keep him: he has a good touch with clients, knows the avenues, but not the honest guardianship of other people's money. It gives me great pleasure to observe him torture himself, battle to stay noble while succumbing to the pleasures of Jacuzzi harems, turning heads in that BMW of his.

Frik intensifies his controls, his methods bordering on draconian even, and profits again go up a further three and half per cent. We pay Maxwell ridiculous bonuses when he least expects it, and then wait for an apology from him. It never comes. I, through a trick I learned from CIA documentaries, from gangster films, surreptitiously hire Raj Govender to secretly audit Frik de Waal, some eleven months of auditing the auditor, at the end of which Raj and I hang our heads in shame: Frik's accounts are bone clean, not a penny out place. Raj, who had come under the pretext of trainee bookkeeper, disappears as swiftly as he had come – never to set foot at the Florentino Ariza again.

Like a fading vocalist gone hoarse, a guitarist ruined by arthritis, a preacher seduced by the sweetness of sin, I sit by the window, on Father's hard chair, and look out to the expansive sea: seagulls rise and dive through a low cloud. I take these breaks from the Remington to calm myself, to stop myself from being alarmed by the great power that seeps from every pore when I am in full swing, when the typewriter keys rattle like machine-gun fire. There is dangerous pleasure in letting go, in complete submission, total engagement with Giovanni and his murderous ways, with Marie and her inviting back. Ships line up in ragged formation on the ocean, silent and patient, ferrying all manner of goods to port, ships that – if I reach for Father's binoculars – bear names such as *Strahlendem Sonnenschein* – Brilliant Sunshine, *Los Tres Reyes Magos* – Three Wise Men, *Tentations de la Nuit* – Temptations of the Night in Abella's tongue, and finally, the fading and rust-eaten *Ernesto Guevara*. There are times when the binoculars sneak up on unforeseen secrets: an oldish couple, visibly drunk, making love on deck, a seagull with a broken wing at the mercy of ocean waves, a sailor throwing up into the sea.

The coffee-shop guest list boasts some eye-catching names: eleven Hollywood A-listers, some royalty who came with bodyguards, and familiar faces on the South African social scene. It warms me, gives me profound joy to receive emails from production companies requesting permission to use Milton Coffees as a movie set; even greater pleasure being invited on set, observing famous actors fluff their lines, flirt, kiss and grope each other behind their trailers. Both the Florentino Ariza and Milton Coffees swarm with customers, more so because Peninsula

Avenue is host to esteemed art galleries and bookshops, to exclusive boutiques and trendy restaurants, on a busy bus route and a shortcut to the airport. Tourists ask how 'Florentino Ariza' ended up on the name plaque of a flower shop in Cape Town. From Father's pet novel, I tell patrons, Marquez's *Love In the Time of Cholera*. None of my beloveds, some of whom have been to my coffee shop, received rare flower arrangements from the Florentino Ariza, or even know that the businesses belong to me, a secret that tickles me greatly. I pretend not to know directions to the coffee shop, arrive late, to Orapeleng's frustration: 'I understand you're not into flowers, but not only is the coffee shop on the main road, it bears your *name*! How ironic! How could you possibly keep getting lost?' I smile, apologise, marvel at how things can be hidden in plain sight.

I park my increasingly unreliable Mercedes, inherited and eighteen years strong, under a streetlamp on a side street, a good five hundred metres from the Florentino Ariza and Milton Coffees, and recline the seat: high enough to maintain a view of my surroundings, but low enough for relative obscurity, for discreet observation. There are two bus stops on this road. Being a main road means heavy vehicular and human traffic, yet channelled so well by town planners that the congestion is not an eyesore, not remotely bothersome. It flows, a stream that mirrors the contours and inclines of the road, collecting human puddles at bus terminals or public phones, at side-street restaurants, and alert show-offs in convertible BMWs and on Ducati motorcycles. Then there are waves of conversation – animated, subdued, hysterical, dramatised – as pedestrians tell their stories to friends, colleagues, companions along the sidewalks.

There is, in this sea of humans, people licking ice creams, kissing, scratching crotches, discarding chewing gum and still-lit cigars, people succumbing to touch and deceits of the senses, pleasured people who to my mind aren't thinking of the Führer right now. The Führer, despite his ambitions, does not occupy a nanosecond of the lives and minds of this sea of people before me. I find it strange that someone who has so marked history should be so readily forgotten, so absent, so insignificant. One would think, wrongly of course, that his kind of ambition and unfathomable evil would have guaranteed him fame into eternity. He is famous, that is for sure, but his is a crippled fame, fame drowned by derision and mockery, famous for being a figure of hatred and, surprisingly, of love. And admiration.

I see, through the window of that same Mercedes, men with forbidding faces, ill-tempered women dragging children across pedestrian crossings and wagging a finger in their faces, a scrawny youth on a motorbike in black leather armed with two pistols and a swastika on his sunburned neck. None of them smile and their coldness penetrates the most loving of people, infecting them with fear, doubt, and finally hatred. Maybe Marie Amsel walks within these crowds? Maybe I will bump into her one day, maybe she is not of a phantom after all. A hint of uncertainty creeps down my spine: the most important thing, surely, would not be whether I bump into her, but whether she would recognise me at once, let me rest my languid arm around her neck, the hand momentarily, as if by accident, brushing her oh-so-majestic nipples, then checking the breast for firmness and arousal. Who would I say I am, Giovanni or Milton? I would choose Milton, because Giovanni will always be a dead end to her, given that he never truly said something about himself, something of value, something that would make Marie pause and take notice. She has a choice, of course, to look through me or avert her gaze, to pass without as much as a feeble nod.

My eyes dart from body to body, bouncing off the elderly and men onto the legs and bottoms of young and seemingly available women, women who, the deeper I think, could have given or received pleasure, received it out of the duty in matrimonial nests and the irritating pleadings of husbands, given it out as torrents of love, the ultimate expression of which was not cooking a sumptuous meal, but yanking their panties off and allowing men to groan and sweat all over them, to let them speak in tongues and commit to out-of-character promises they could never keep. That is what pleasure does to people: it distorts them.

I spot two examples of those distorted: Alexis and her banker husband walk hand in hand towards Milton Coffees, sit and order cake all the while warped in their own web of intimacy. Ignorance is the great leveller here: me not knowing what they did this morning, for example, and them not knowing that Milton Coffees belongs to me – oblivious to the nude man sitting in the S500 Mercedes with tinted windows, binoculars in hand. I don't know how I feel or what to feel seeing Alexis like that; see her totally invest herself in a man, a man thoughtful enough to open and close those white SAAB doors for her, bend to his knees to tie her shoelaces, stand to kiss her between the eyes. That man who rubs his nose against hers, who pulls her chair out at Milton Coffees, and when Cape Town weather changes, the man who throws a scarf around her neck – and not only that, but arranges it in such a manner that not even the slightest chill finds its way into a pore of her bosom. Unlike me, this man has taken the time to dress up: shirt and tie, shoes polished, hair and moustache trimmed in a way he knows represent him best. It is not hard to see that he listens with empathy and understanding, his head completely cleared of the commotion and distractions of Peninsula Avenue, entirely focused on my former lover.

There is a stab of jealousy, of course, of wishing all manner of calamities upon him (scurvy, the most intense and incurable strain of madness that exists above all the others, sudden and permanent loss of bladder control – and, most importantly, erectile dysfunction so complete and irreversible that his only option would be to follow Bull to the train tracks or seek a life of spiritual enlightenment and obedience away from temptations of intercourses of the body on faraway continents). But scurvy did not get him – none of the other calamities did – for I see through the binoculars Alexis' hand cover his manly paws with manicured claws, a gesture that prompts him to bare his fangs in delight. It is clear to me that he has no ambition, feeding on the leftovers of others. Look at him, the simpleton grinning and chewing my cake like a tortoise. Where is Lee Harvey Oswald when justifiable assignments arise? I notice how Alexis arches her back, how her hips balance distances to her knees to the front and her rump, how her smile bathes everything around her in magnetic light. That banker toad does not know it yet, but if he ever loses her that scent of hers will haunt him to his grave. Women don't smell like Alexis because of beautifications and perfume deceptions – they do so in spite of them!

I have a good mind to leave the Mercedes engine running, leisurely walk along the sidewalk towards them, blending into

PLEASURE

that sea of humans, and on reaching their table, crack his fucking skull open with these binoculars – then speed off to Casablanca Estates, take the lift all the way to the roof terrace on the fortieth floor and declare my resurrected love until I grow hoarse, sparking a televised hostage negotiation standoff to last eighteen hours. And when negotiators change shifts, when hope is restored, jump off the roof because living without Alexis would have never been my intention to start with. Brains on the tarmac below. A smudge. A stain. Like Bull's.

You have not seen Alexis smile, seen her sleepy and dozing, seen her fresh out of the shower, her torso and head wrapped in white towels. You have not seen her eat pasta, tie her shoelaces. You have not seen her at the mercy of influenza, her nostrils reddened, eyes teary, her voice nasal and throaty. You have not seen her just from an important meeting (navy suit, white shirt), seen her undress: suit jacket then shirt then bra; seen brassier lines on her delicate skin, leaving it a faded hue of burgundy. You have not seen her walk around the apartment in only her skirt, her upper body bare, watched kettle steam rise and mist her nipples as she attends to coffee cravings. You have not, mystified and electrocuted, seen her go out of her way to offer seductive theatrics; never seen her in a state of undress for more than was necessary. You have never seen her dance, stoop to touch her toes, rest her heel on the bed and bend to kiss her own knee, or witness her purr to the pleasure of strawberries dipped in cream. To see her iron and double check her blouses was revelatory, but to stand behind her, crotch planted firmly against her apple bottom, my manly hand cupping hers over the iron's handle, my mouth adorning her neck with light, evenly spaced kisses was the greatest feeling one can ever wish for. You have never heard her, when dismissing over-eager hands, a mouth determined to swallow her whole, say: 'Not today, my Blue Sky. I have new steps to learn.' Blue Sky. That infinite, vacuous, unfathomable thing that all can see but never touch. Much like pleasure.

It is not her immaculate navel or industrious wrists that so moved me to the brink of tears, or even when I discovered, was told in passing, that she and two dancer friends had a soup kitchen for the homeless – a soup kitchen I now spend time at in her honour. That is not the main reason I weep into pillows in my lonesome, why I fling coffee mugs against walls in rage, why I sit staring at the sea for hours on end: I realised, quite late, that she wouldn't know how *not* to be noble even if she tried, that there was with her a rarer form of intercourse not easily known or experienced: that of the soul. My wanting to bash that banker over the head with Father's binoculars is not a rage to win back lusts – far from it; it is the realisation that what I have lost is incalculable: her humanness.

It is overcast, an afternoon of low-hanging clouds, an illusion of moving mist crawling over the sea. I cannot see the sea, but can hear it, its low-key and sustained dirge: a weeping for Marie, for my brother Bull, sorrow for the Africans of the Congo and of everywhere, some maimed and owned by Leopold and his *Force*

Publique – mules for rubber, for their brothers and sisters stolen before them, their stillborn offspring, sickly and weakened bodies drowned in the high seas, their names as many as the stars that adorn the night skies: Africans who became niggers on America's plantations and in the Führer's backyard: Bastards of Rhineland. Peculiar. Strange. Monstrously strange.

There is nothing more to be done for my manuscript now, except that in literature, Father once said, in writing, what one perceives to be the end of things is often not even the beginning, that what one imagines to be Everest might not even be a meadow. It is strange, I know, but my nude toils in front of the Remington have drained me of passion, reducing me to a nudist who spies on Capetonians from behind curious curtains, pointing binoculars at a lost and homeless dog narrowly missed by a city bus, the evocative names given to boats and ships cruising by, young couples fondling each other under tables at side-street coffee shops when they think not a soul sees them, and pickpockets going about their trade. I see women; women see me. I am not sure if they know about the intercourse of the soul, and if they do, whether they would be prepared to be courted by a nudist who is finding it increasingly hard to put on clothes.

I cannot say what the exact benefit of my state of undress is – I don't think it can be reduced to logic – and have resolved not to interrogate the issue any further, to accept it for the freedom that nudity ushers. How liberating to be able to witness sweat beads form on one's self, to sniff like an animal one's armpits on those humid evenings when the sea is at its calmest, when aircraft engines punctuate the night peace. It is another question entirely that persists, taunts me: what do you know about pleasure? It has taken me many months of staring at the sea, my soul coiled in knots, crying on the kitchen floor at losing Alexis, waking to find curtains drenched by rain and steaming in the mid-morning sun. The wooden floor around the window is beginning to suffer: rainwater damage from windows forgotten wide open overnight, wine stains and cigarette burns, ants congregating around apple cores. The wet wood is beginning to bulge into an uneven slope, making sitting there on chairs wobbly and risky business. The last straw is when I sleep through a brief but brutal storm to wake to a heap of hailstones hurled through the open window onto the floor.

And so I sit by the window gazing at the sea. With sweeping languid movements, my eyes hop from ship to seagull, from seagull to cloud, cloud to airplane, airplane back to sea. Another piece of the puzzle falls into place: over and above *balance*, the dictates of *conscience* have limited or no place in the realm of pleasure in its *purest* form. One can nurse a jolt of lame guilt for peripheral pleasures – Marie with her sensual back in that bathtub, for instance – but a certain ruthlessness, a particular primal charge is demanded when an Abella decides to sit on your face. No literature can ever explain that, contain or illuminate it. It seems to me that that universe, of sitting on faces, does not belong on Remington keys. It seems no amount of wine or fasting or weeping or staring at the sea or Marie dreams will crystallise the fusion of suffering and bliss lurking in every pleasure encounter: a lone, then strange woman (Alexis) artfully eating pasta; Abella, a French muse whose first words upon meeting were 'Hello, my name is Professor Beaudrie and I teach things to do with sensations', and when I requested an example, she responded with: '*La langue est titulaire d'innombrables clés de plaisir.*'– The tongue holds countless keys to pleasure. And continued: '*Ce doit être vrai que lécher un cœur est l'expression suprême de l'amour, de la sensation. Mais les cœurs sont cachés dans les cages thoraciques, alors nous léchons et suçons les orteils, les lobes d'oreilles, les nombrils – même les globes oculaires.*' – It must be that licking a heart is the ultimate expression of love, of sensation. But hearts are hidden away in rib cages, so we lick and suck on toes, earlobes, navels – even eyeballs; or Masechaba throwing her head back in delight, exclaiming: '*Ona le lepona le lepila*, my baby.' – You look good naked, my love. And 'My God, Milton – all penises should look like yours. It is a delightful sight, almost edible'; or Bull who, when stoned to Pluto, loved saying that it is utterly useless living without a little danger.

My Remington toils, and yet my expeditions into the mind have not led me to a conclusive answer of what pleasure is or isn't. They have instead meant only a long-winded descent into treasure troves and ruins buried amid the very shadows of my soul. What should have been a silent prayer, a brief observation of a moment of silence for Bull ended up stretching for days on end, days that became confused: I never knew whether I was mourning Bull or weeping for Alexis. So loud my sobs must have got that a shadow paused in the sliver of light creeping in from under the door, and a quavering voice, no doubt that of an elderly woman, inquired: 'Whose child weeps so bitterly, without a comforter?' I sat up from the floor, wiped my tears, held my breath, until I heard her shuffle away, muttering: 'What is this world coming to?'

Alexander, or a man who calls himself Alexander, who could be anybody really – Gilbert, Nicolas or Paul – a man generally considered insane, a man with big liquid brown eyes and a face hidden behind a greying beard, stalks Milton Coffees. He is tall, homeless but without being pitiful, pointing to some unreliable, on-and-off hospitality from well-wishers: those with afflicted consciences that fizzle halfway when they discover the burdens that come with being merciful return to their known but comfortable selfish ways.

Very tall men, like fat men, tend to have compromised posture and suspect locomotion. Not Alexander. He struts the streets like a redwood, his bald patch gleaming with perspiration, earlobes and nostrils all hair. Tufts of hair also cover his chest like a golf green, complemented by a Tolstoy beard that hides his rosy cheeks and pink lips, a smallish mouth from which words roll with guarded defiance in an almost undetectable lisp. His rapid blinking points to a history of a stammer or a furious temper that has waned, leaving only flustered checks whenever provoked. A deep, rounded voice in laughter and speech, a voice that could have earned him prestige in opera recitals, gave him somewhat misplaced authority.

Before I knew him, took pity on him, I said he could be served at Milton Coffees whenever he wanted. He looked puzzled, then confused, then irritated and said the most unexpected thing by a homeless person, spoken not with an exaggerated sense of self-pity but from a position of great power. He looked me square in the eyes without malice or anger and, as if dazed, as if emerging out of a seventy-year trance, said: 'Why do you treat me no respect? Who asked you for anything?' I was not sure whether to be offended or bewildered, and feeling stung, shot back: 'Fresh food will always be better than eating out of garbage bins.'

'Don't be so sure,' he fired back. 'Your sympathies lack foresight.'

'Meaning what, exactly?'

'Well ...' he said without blinking, 'coffee has never been isolated as a benefit in life. It stains your teeth, keeps some of us awake. Are you saying you are also prepared to pay for my dental procedures? Will you write down your address so I can trace you when caffeine denies me sleep, rest? Once there, will I be free to curl up in your bed, help myself to your shaving blades, your favourite pair of pyjamas? What do we do if your coffee triggers and worsens my ulcers, if I am in pain and need hospitalisation? You see what I mean? You have not thought your offer through – it is very impulsive and not in your best interests, which is a long-winded and perhaps complicated way to say I respectfully decline your offer, as it will worsen rather than lighten my burdens.' He shuffled away, and was gone.

But he always returns, Alexander. The greatest pleasure is sitting behind the car's tinted windows, Father's binoculars in hand, spying on him and the world. The Führer will never walk the streets of Cape Town. Strangely, disarmingly, perplexing, it is, even here in Cape Town and Johannesburg, trains that ferry the faceless and silent around the metropolis, to their eighteen-hour toils in Bishopscourt and Cape Town's factories. But here there are no Eichmann men with torches and dogs at the end of each train trip, officers with makeshift registration stations to record victims, to meticulously ask: name, surname, trade. One never knows what the metropolis will do, because it has proven itself to be willing to do just about anything to its citizens, worse things than chewing and spitting them out. I continue to see Alexander, watch him stalk patrons at Milton Coffees, expose himself to both men and women – not because of any base desire, but because that is the only power he knows he has: the power to shock and disgust, to unsettle, offend. It is futile calling the police. One officer, a regular who in her irritation and helplessness forgets the law, asks me: 'You going to waste my time – waste state resources – every time this Alexander prances about naked? What crime are we to charge him with? Because he won't know the difference anyway … Don't you see this man is unwell?'

Alexander listens intently, a big grin adorning his face, and without missing a heartbeat responds: '*Unwell?* Who told you that? Because I touch myself here and choose to show some people what I have? It's not like I spend my whole life penis flashing – for that would be an insult to me and what I stand for.'

'What *do* you stand for?' asks Constable Pistorius.

'Me?'

'Yes, you – and please put that thing back in your pants. Do you not see there are ladies around here?'

'I see the ladies, all right, but I am not doing it for them – not to impress or annoy them.'

'Ladies don't like men who do what you doing.'

'That's their problem. I am not doing it for them.'

'Do you not want a lady of your own, a family, and maybe you can do what you are doing in private?'

'No. No ladies. What for?'

'Love. Friendship. Companionship. *Geselskap?*'

'No. I have no need for any of that. I want to be left alone to stand for my own things.'

'What is it that you stand for exactly?' asks Pistorius.

'I don't know. What do you think I stand for?'

'You tell me. You the one doing the standing for something – what is it?'

'I don't drink or smoke or do drugs.'

'Is that what you stand for then?'

'No. I don't stand for any of that.'

'Let's get going. You are disturbing the pea—'

'I stand for anything that makes sense to me. If a bird eats out of my hand, I can choose to stand for it. If a hungry thief steals and succeeds, I might stand for him or the police or the bread he stole. Or not stand for any of them. I can stand for your dog if you want. Is this dog yours?'

'No. It belongs to the Police Department. It's government property.'

Alexander frowned: 'The government owns dogs?'

'Yes, it does.'

'I can't stand for their dogs this year. Maybe next year.'

'You just stand for things randomly?'

'No. Not randomly. You think I'm stupid?'

'Not at all. Just curious.'

'I stand when I want, because it makes me happy. I say to whatever or whoever: I stand for you. Or I protest. If these coffee drinkers offended me, I wouldn't stand for them. I would break these coffee-shop windows. I might, if you offend me, decide to let you go. Or take the dog from you. You will tell the government why you lost its property.'

'This is not just a dog. It's Officer Maples from the Canine Unit.'

'You have completely lost your marbles. A dog is a policewoman?'

Milton Coffees patrons cannot help but laugh – laughter that gladdens Alexander – and, big grin still on his face, he simply shuffles away, oblivious to the world around him.

It bothers me that Alexander, or whatever his name is, who does not have to slave on a Remington, reflecting on and explaining things, who without bothering to take a bath or contributing meaningfully to the Cape Town metropolis, wields such abundant power, that he can wield it however excessively without any real repercussions. It is not only his power to shock and offend, but the vastness of it all, its complete lack of boundaries, the total disregard for millennia of civilisations. I cannot confirm whether Alexander is aware of his power: the ability to exist outside of human wants and desires, to disregard pleasure entirely, for it not to exist or affect anything, to be of no consequence, neither sought nor yearned for, not even perceived. Which, if even remotely true, means that pleasure is inferior to madness, that madness is the ultimate leveller, that life is quite bearable without the dictates of perspective. It is perspective that can save or ruin things: lives brought into sharp focus or dimmed, SAAB doors opened or ignored, Alexander refusing to commit to anything he might want to embrace and defend, the eternal changing of his mind.

I wonder, of course, if he has heard of or knows anything about the Führer, if he would stand for or against him. He is, in a way, a kindred spirit; all my slaving over the Remington is in the nude, after all – only I do not flash my privates at anyone, because I have neither the inclination nor courage to do so, and because I, generally considered sane, would not risk being jailed or fined for indecent exposure. One needs rock-solid defence against the law. It is not enough to use scorching temperatures as an excuse for getting naked, for instance. One must have, or at least present, a compelling argument on the need to do away with clothes, to – when confronted – offer the most perplexing and reasonable reason to be a nuisance. Publicly judges invoke the law, but privately they must wonder, even secretly admire the likes of Alexander for their fortitude, their disregard for order.

My distress with Alexis is straightforward: I want to die being able to say, I have loved in my life – truly loved, been molten and cooled and hammered by love, cast and polished. I want to say I know what transformative love is – abundant love, a love that glows and sparkles and vibrates, a love that dwells momentarily on each spinal vertebrae, warming it with just enough heat to evoke giddiness. A kind of love that can breathe under water, bleed but never die, a love that can draw trillions of lines that connect stars – lines destined for the heart of the beloved in all her imperfections. The wounds won't heal by themselves.

It is with a tinge of bitterness that I learn that no lasting enlightenment has come from my inquiry, that my toils on the Remington have produced little by way of insight into the ways and deceptions of pleasure but a tame realisation that there is no art without life and that life is not easily distilled into art. There were false sparks, sure, shooting stars that promised guidance, guidance that never came; distortions of reality that have no doubt maimed my manuscript. Maybe that is how reality works – in distortions, in extremes; maybe balance was never an ingredient of reality or pleasure, maybe reality and pleasure can only truly exist because they are so illuminated by extremes. Only the crudest events make their mark on history. Only the unreachable and unobtainable have the power to elevate or dwarf lives. Only the most daunting of deeds ever produce anything worth living for: Marie Amsel's moonlit back, reading great poets in graveyards, the Storming of the Bastille, that ash that descended silently over the Reich.

I don't dream of Marie Amsel any more. In fact, that was the one and only time I did. And yet I continue to look for her in Cape Town's multitudes, discreetly study every face that resembles hers, curvatures of waists of women her size, and those reddened, sorrowful and weepy eyes. It is impossible, I know, for if she truly existed Marie would not be a sight to behold at at least a hundred and three: dry skin, runny nose perhaps, droopy breasts. She would not spark in me that buzz of lust that echoed in my very bone marrow, for she would be dead or senile, indifferent to the urges of time and desire and manly charms. She would be worried about aches, joints that won't bend, about being unable to tie her own shoelaces, all her drooling onto well-wishers. But there – right there at the centre of her pupils, with their fading glimmer, a momentary spark that flashes when something jolts her memory – would be all her girl stories written in tears, the distance and duration to her grave calculated according to doctors' estimations, a wondering mind that would have lost the ability to choose and compare, to dismiss without finality for a crisper perspective come morning. There would be no distinction between morning and night, but a world drained of its thrills and pleasures, existing in blurry shadows, cruel monotones. I would not want to see her in any bath; would avert my gaze at the slightest hint of her intending to undress and, without saying so, wonder why I was so unlucky to witness such overwhelming imperfections. Bodies are like that; they invite witnesses, then judge them if the bodies are too old. How dare you look at Marie Amsel like that? She is old enough to be your great-grandmother. Have you no shame!

The Culture Institute is a beautiful building: bluish glass and polished aluminium, lit by low-hanging yellow spotlights suspended on rusty chains. The reception areas boast all manner of art installations: a Wall Street-type bull, Venda snake dance, Mandela looking serene. The hallways and lecture halls are adorned with oils on canvas from South Africa's rural provinces. My sabbatical ends in a week; a week that, like others past, is sure to feel as long as months stretched into a haunting haze of loneliness and Remington toils.

I have asked myself another question to which I am still unable to arrive at a satisfactory, or even convincing answer: how does one, if I cannot even pin down pleasure in a five-hundred-page tome, teach culture to rotten wretches born poisoned: the institute's hungover Mohawk-haired poets in orange shoes carrying acoustic guitars they cannot play, reserved and lonesome potheads whose contribution to society is silence and self-conscious smiles, the Porsche- and BMW-driving sons of CEOs who eyeball me and call me a punk in the Institute parking lot, gum-chewing sadists who block out my lectures with Led Zeppelin and Kanye West on headphones, their pleasure dials perpetually turned to maximum in every aspect of their lives. It is like talking to trees. The only decent response I have witnessed – or at least flutters of it – is when we did a module on music videos as vehicles for cultural expression: music videos all about Bentleys and beds and breasts shoved into camera lenses, young things salaciously licking red lollipops with matching lipstick, the opening and shutting of legs to thudding rhythm-and-blues beats. What's *cultural* about that? I saw faces light up, even the most defeated in my flock sit up, though any real insights remained elusive as words thrown around included *hot*, *da bomb* (spelled that way, why?), *off the hook*, and *sick* to denote what serious scholars would mystify as *aesthetics*. I doubt that my flock is teachable, because to them culture is rebellion and showing off – because the gory SMS I intercept when it becomes clear that there is mobile phone whoring underway tells me that the boys and young women who jump onto their backs and whisper things into their ears can only lead to early and sudden departures from my lectures.

It must not be forgotten that Abella was a whole human being, that her life, her being and existence were not limited to her erotic whispers, competing with my younger lovers – the 'Two Little Mice' – and on very special and far-between days, sitting on my face.

Waiting for pleasures to manifest, to mature, to ripen can itself be a pleasurable thing. That wait – the impatience and angst and excitement that gives it its sweet discomforts, the playing around with and distorting of time – is one of the greatest pleasures there is: not knowing anything for sure, misreading hints, being pleasantly surprised. In a sense, or perhaps despite sense, Abella's sensuality defines her, but one has to know her really well to know that besides being a gifted and dedicated teacher, she makes the most horrid coffee in the universe, that she is one of the bravest people alive (kills spiders, does cartwheels in front of slow traffic, firmly believes that the last number on vehicle speedometers is a goal to be achieved), and is too generous by earthly standards, too selfless without being aware. It is tragic that fleeting encounters with strangers must leave them with the wrong impressions: that she is flirtatious and possibly even sluttish, which would be rushed and untrue. Abella despises groupie behaviour and, though overly generous in most other aspects of her life, it takes some work, endless time, patience and charm by the bucketful for her to even consider bedroom rituals.

I remember all too well many aborted attempts, many detours, countless carnal tipping points halted at the very last second, numerous discussions and assurances and future considerations that needed convincing and prompt answers, at the end of which I would, frustrated and inspired, say: 'I understand that these things do and should take time, but you can at least show me your breasts, no?'

She would blush, smile, and surprise me with a complex rendition of a 'No' I will never forget: *'Ne sois pas méchant. Les seins ne poussent pas sur les arbres.'* – Don't be naughty. Breasts don't grow on trees.

It was an unwinnable battle to convince Abella to surrender her body without a hundred questions and countless counter proposals of being only friends and holding hands and kissing, with sensual explorations restricted to neck nibbling and lower-back rubbing, open palms allowed to momentarily rest motionless on fully clothed buttocks without the option of massaging or squeezing, such that we stood pained and breathless, as if struck by forked lightning. So, after those multiple lightning strikes, we stood dazed in lust, as if overwhelmed by the smell of sulphur from our lightning-wrecked bodies, revolting against our futile restraints against love, courtship and fucking – so much so that I died countless small deaths, some brief, some elaborate. It is shocking, I know, but there were moments when I gave up – thought there should be a difference between desire and making a fool out of oneself and, sulking and apparently indifferent, I would sit myself down in front of the Remington and hammer at the keys, birthing disjointed and pathetic prose. Abella would sense this, of course, sense my possible loss of interest and promptly realise that manly interest in women has its own currency, that one can be left emotionally destitute if certain and carefully selected men are not given keys to the Bastille, that the motives and procedures should never be so cumbersome as to cause fatal distress, that the withholding of the keys should take into account the possibility of a sudden and unexpected death – that life is too short and unpredictable, that denial of certain privileges must never include covert encouragements, that a 'no' should mean a 'no' and not 'you can touch my bum' in freeze frame.

That got me thinking about Eichmann and Himmler and the rest of them: if you are to commit such a sordid crime of that heartlessness and magnitude, is it not unfair to shroud your actions in cowardice too, to cover up things and misrepresent facts, to, even with absolute and unquestionable power, see the need to deceive, to sugar coat, to conceal? Think about it: seventeen million people, informed that they would be enslaved and starved and gassed and shot at random, are not going to sit on their laurels or volunteer to board trains destined for Auschwitz and other camps. They are not, if they fully comprehend the magnitude of their dilemma, their impeding extinction, going to turn the other cheek. They would have rebelled, shouted until they were hoarse – and with them a world that would not have wasted bombs on critical but useless targets, for the true targets, those that really mattered, those that would have shaped the nature and focus of the war, those that would define history for histories to come, were those fucking labour and extermination camps.

Abella could not have known that the clanking of the Remington keys explored these thoughts – and feeling vulnerable (ignored), said: '*Quelle est la proportion amour-contre-luxure dans cette poursuite à toi? Est-ce que c'est le coup de foudre ou veux-tu tout simplement arriver à tes fins avec moi? Dis-moi, je pourrais peut-être l'envisager, ne plus me tenir sur mes gardes. Mais il faut que je sois certaine.*' – What is your love-to-lust ratio in this chase of yours? Is it a question of thunderous love or do you just want to have your way with me? Tell me, I just might consider it, let my guard down. But I have to be sure.

And when I continued to sulk, continued to bang away on the Remington – despite every nerve-ending stretching to breaking point at the possibility that she was finally relenting – she buried me in an avalanche that was at once a veiled threat, an offer and a warning: '*Tu ne peux pas être puéril et bouder au sujet de mon corps. Je finirai par ne plus te baiser du tout si tu te conduis mal.*' – You cannot be childish and sulk about my body. I will end up not 'giving you some' at all if you misbehave.

That is what she said – and added, with a rather classy and bloody literary reference, that I should 'Beware the Ides of March', which was both heart-warming and scary. Heart-warming because it was said with the most pleasant of smiles; scary because 'beware' is not a word generally associated with the erotic. So it was that March fifteenth came – and with it the delicate, entirely unexpected, humbling, and bordering on profound privilege of deflowering Abella at the ripe age of thirty-six, one drizzly evening on Father's noisy bed, an act that was not only intense but transformative. How she gasped in pleasure and, it has to be said, a little pain, and barely audible, below her breath, whispered: '*Mon Dieu! Il est tout à fait vrai. Il n'y a rien à comparer aux rapports sexuels dans quatre univers pas encore créés!*' –

My God! It is all true. There is nothing like intercourse in four universes yet to be created!

Before they became marital poisons, my disagreements with Orapeleng were mild, harmless altercations that at worst triggered temporary irritation, sulking with brief life spans, discomforts that could and did melt away at the smallest apology from the offending party, or even just a hint of an apology encoded in unexpected courtesies. She would cook roast beef, for instance, open a bottle of my favourite Merlot, and wear that see-through dress that reminded me that she was not perfect but necessary. Vain arguments over sitcom plots and snoring transgressions, scowls over who of the world's top tennis players was both talented and cute, unkind words uttered in truth, frustration and jest about delinquents in our respective families: her spinster sister Margo, who never tired of pinching my bum when no one was looking, or my brother Bull who swindled her of thousands of rands through carefully crafted and impenetrable emotional blackmail. It was years before I found out – and only after pressing her to explain why she suddenly disliked, even hated my brother. And then she witnessed Margo and her bum-pinching passions during a family picnic in August some years ago and, infuriated, accused me of doing things behind her back.

'You are worse than a pig,' she charged. 'There is nothing you can do or say; not say or not do that will ever explain you allowing Margo anywhere near you knowing she is a man-eater! Whatever explanation, however elaborate, means nothing before you even think or say it. You are weak and cannot be trusted!'

I was livid, and said some rather dramatic and corrosive things myself, but things that in hindsight were nonetheless true – then and now. Mild arguments thus became frosty withdrawals and silences, sieges and counter sieges worsened to unexplained and sudden disappearances that with time resulted in Orapeleng crashing our Honda and breaking two ribs, while in the company of an intoxicated and clearly smug Pule – an orthodontist who clearly had unauthorised access to and benefits from my wife. She said she would leave him, but my response was brutal if not original.

'You are worse than a pig,' I said, calmly. 'There is nothing you can do or say; not say or not do that will ever explain you allowing Pule anywhere near you knowing that he is a man! Whatever explanation, however elaborate, means nothing before you even think or say it. You are weak and cannot be trusted!' After all, I had proof, solid proof, on the home answering machine, of that cocky and obviously suicidal idiot saying: 'Thanks for last night, sugar. My balls are still sore.'

That was when I made my way to Casablanca Estates, wounded and in despair, to share my burdens with Father. He listened without comment for three days and long evenings; he listened and on the fourth day said: 'Those are not the only balls wrecking marriages and lives, Milton. The statistics are too disturbing to contemplate. You have balls too. Use them. Between us, there must be something you have done that has made Orapeleng vengeful and insecure. Women don't just open their legs like that, that easily. But it is too late now. Do you really want to live your life thinking about and imagining sore balls? Every man is and should be responsible for his own; refrain from thinking what other men do with theirs. Better said than done, of course, but that is the brutal truth. So, what are you going to do?'

I did not have an answer for him, but knew for certain that I did not want to spend my life thinking about the anatomies of rivals: sadistic, intemperate, depraved bastards. It is amazing what complications an 'innocent' pinch of the buttocks can unleash in the realm of pleasure.

Because it looks so normal, so ordinary, so expected, it is not immediately evident that people get chewed up by the metropolis: overworked taxi drivers, starved night watchmen armed with batons, street-corner cobblers way past retirement age. As Cape Town dishes its seductions and cruelties in accordance with history's ruins, as I doze by the window gazing at the sea, my life becomes about *omission* rather than *commission*: deliberate subtractions, the ruthless doing away with things.

The matrimonial house is signed off to Orapeleng, Father's furniture is all but gone, my three beloveds have also been cut loose, and the midnight knocks have long ceased. Zaid Moosa Motors has offered me a pitiful amount for Father's Mercedes. Paperwork is advanced for Milton Coffees and the Florentino Ariza, sale agreements to Ghanaian investors. My resignation letter is written and signed, to be delivered to the Head of Institute within seventy-two hours, via a courier service. The manuscript is done – except, of course, for the ending, or the beginning of the ending. Or an ending that never begins.

Pleasure. Who would have thought that a single word could be so sought, so slippery, so flammable as to alter and ruin lives? All my clothes are gone to old-age homes and orphanages, shoes, everything. I have butchered the telephone line, drowned the answering machine in a sink of boiling water. My entire music collection, twenty-six years' worth, and books boasting countless literary gems have been donated to the city library. Every conceivable personal record has been destroyed: childhood pictures, university and medical records, photographs of Ilze-Marie and Zoë – my university flames – my passport, an old King James Bible someone gifted me, brassieres in three colours and sizes, publishing contracts and personal letters spanning twenty-one years, a lone, water-damaged picture of Mother, souvenirs from the northern and western hemispheres. There had also been a long list of other important and not-so-important items: medications for chronic ulcers and irritable bowel syndrome, the Remington, eight boxes containing Second World War history and pictorials, a picture of a seated and suited Führer looking out an elevated window at the *Wolfschanze* drinking tea, pots and pans and dishes – effectively leaving only those hideous burgundy curtains and the unfinished manuscript.

Two years of staring at the sea pass, and with them a deepening sense of blurry enlightenment about life and its secrets. I, technically speaking, own nothing, other than leather pants and a white silk shirt. I think: what is the greatest pleasure of them all? It depends.

I have, for a considerable fee, committed daring fraud.

Meetings in obscure pubs, in dingy cafés, and several thousands of rands have secured me a legitimate death certificate, of natural causes, and a cremation seven days later. My accomplice and fellow fraudster has, via his extended networks, ensured that I have no official document of whatever kind; that everything is wound down, that I am, technically and bureaucratically, dead; 'deceased' is the official word, as a result of deep-vein thrombosis.

There was some pleasure in attending one's own cremation, at which the presiding priest casually enquired whether *I* knew the deceased, to which I answered without batting an eyelid: 'You could say that. But not too well.' How impressive his knowledge of procedure, my masterful accomplice, who gave my cremation service such dignity: the giant candles, the pink-and-white tulips in ceramic vases, the hired choir and an assortment of his associates standing in for family and friends. It was liberating, a great pleasure seeing that pricy casket, a purplish brown artwork of a thing, slowly pushed into the flames, my supposed mortal remains (in effect, Father's papers spanning fifty-three years) consumed by fire. I sat there, motionless, with a peculiar sense of being alive, singing hymns I knew, humming those I didn't. The priest read from Matthew and Revelations – scriptures about pain and loss and eternal life, about the end of days and the burdens of sin. It was a moving sermon – so moving, in fact, that I shed a few tears for myself, too deeply touched not to be affected.

A silence descends on the apartment, and with it an overwhelming sense of entanglement with the imperfections of the universe. I am slowly ridding myself of ownership of things, one item at a time. I will continue until all that is left is my breath, without which I would *truly* be dead. It brings a certain guilty peace, a deafening calm, this arrangement – this being unreachable, dissolving into thin air, subtracting oneself from the universe.

But there is one picture I cannot bring myself to part with: it is of a child, a boy of about six, Polish, walking on a sidewalk dragging a dismembered kite while the Führer's armies march in tight formation in the background. What became of him, I ask myself, and what dreams and yearnings formed in his vacant eyes, a posture that hints at distress. Perhaps he ended up in Geneva somewhere, authored important treaties governing the world, lived to old age. Maybe he ended as ash in Giovanni Gomez's coffee.

With this unburdening of the self behind me, I sleep, sometimes for days on end, without a single dream, to be woken by hunger or thirst, at times thunderclaps from freak and sudden storms. I have discarded everything I owned, everything believed in, have become feather light and feel as if light can travel through me, illuminate my deepest wells. I still sit, for hours sometimes, gazing at the sea, without thoughts or emotions. I am no different from a flowerpot, a wristwatch, or a cigarette pack left next to the window, a lifeless object without the slightest yearning. I don't wonder, perceive or reflect, just sit immobilised by calm, so quiet I can almost hear my hair grow. Maybe new beliefs will come, new urges, new people. Or maybe old people in new guises, with stronger convictions. Alexis, maybe. There is a distant prick, a blunt jolt of a faded thought, distant, too distant, too unformed to be of any use, of consequence: is this what true revolution is, a revolt against oneself, against existence itself, letting it be whatever it wants to be without me, without me second guessing what will or might happen?

Is it this *ultimate* revolution, this indifference to the universe, that is perhaps the greatest discovery, the avenue to the *source* and not the *symptoms* of pleasure? I have, all of my life, mistaken pleasure for sensation. It is more than that, my brooding tells me; it is the power to choose: what to see, what and whom to touch, how ferociously or delicately. In its purest form, pleasure is *not* habitual surrender to the senses; it is how to disregard them, to reorder them according to one's whims, to control the nature and duration of one's encounters with pleasure. Some pleasures last for decades, even lifetimes, while others are shallow and fleeting. Because pleasures are many and varied, it makes no sense living whole lives imprisoned by their unpredictable appearances, their shadows, their heating and cooling for no good reason. Great are pleasures that are yet to arrive, to be known, their powers guessed and estimated – sampled one throb at a time. Great, because pleasures already known have already died, have become routine, parasitic, unreliable. Dead. Like the false beauty of stars, light corpses adorning night skies. It may be disconcerting but no less true that pleasures are at their most beautiful when dead – little more than corpses occupying too much space. There is no greater feeling, no more momentous pleasure than a complete lack of existence and accountability: to live without living, outside the trappings of tangibility and foolishness.

Father's apartment, with that intoxicating view of the sea, is the last to go. On Barrack Street, in the heart of the old semi-industrial zone, there is an old factory shop, one of those three-storey brick eyesores with foundations dug into the bowels of the earth, its windows distorting street views of people's knees and vehicle tyres. I see other things too, sliced and confined by the window dimensions: raindrops, moving patches of blue and red police and ambulance lights, walking sticks trembling and tapping by. There are calves of women, only calves and no feet, no shoes, a distorted but rather amusing study of human locomotion.

The basement room is dark and musty, with a worn green carpet. The place bears multiple histories, witness to a parade of inhabitants that predate me: a pair of large man construction-type boots caked with cement, the soles held together by wire, a pink plastic water gun stained black by ink, half-finished landscape paintings with severe water damage, and a lone cartridge from a spent bullet. There are other hints of other histories too: hypodermic needles, whisky bottles, and a dirty magazine. I live here now, in a neglected factory area of town, where I burrow and hide in plain sight, for R200 a month. I have inherited a two-plate stove, which overheats and trips the electricity, and use one pot to cook and heat meals. I have a mattress, some reliable blankets, and two nails on the wall on which I hook my leather pants when that need to be in the nude beckons me. I am not lonely; I have street sounds above me – voices, cars, footsteps, seldom birds – and am too busy weaning my soul of impurities to be sad. I desire nothing and no one, burrow with my manuscript and pencils, tracing my thought patterns.

PLEASURE

My landlord, a Mr Knoppel, vulture-beaked and dwarfish, collects his rent erratically and, I suppose, on a needs basis. I don't complain about anything, ignore the leaking toilet, the cracked window, the battered ceiling. It is clear that this was a printing works, evidenced by the defunct presses, the congealed ink canisters, tuberculosis awareness posters left uncollected. There is no Remington here, no sea view, no curtains. The sunrise is harsh and blinding, my pleasure euthanasia's numbing, my thinking lucid some of the time. How intoxicating this state of nonexistence, of burrowing; how pleasurable it is existing above mundane life pleasures, this total erasure of oneself, this lurking in the shadows, this counting bread slices, this reading one's newspaper obituaries in all their confusions and splendour. When my lungs threaten to ache, I crawl out of my burrow once a month, in the dead of night, for ten minutes of clean air. My surroundings are deserted: defunct diesel pumps, undecided ruins, ghost factories, sporadic nests for the stoned and homeless. I walk back to my burrow, slow, but at times briskly, for there are times when I sense I am being followed, when a sudden chill runs down my spine, when I have to bite my tongue to remind myself that I am still alive. When the lights are off – those yellowish lights from stained overhead light covers, flickering as to induce a daze – it is very dark in my burrow. And yet it is the darkness we must seek, not the light, for light fools the eyes that they see, when it is in fact our *minds* that do. I have achieved great things staring at the darkness, when before, during and after my meditations I will myself to see the sea as I had for many years from Father's apartment window, added Pyramids of Giza to the Cape Town skyline, even stopped the Führer from committing suicide.

My burrowing is not imprisonment, not quite, and not exile, not really, not a pilgrimage nor hiding, not even isolation. It is a journey into the *essence* of things. Solitude. Quietude. Enlightenment. It is a search not for discovery, but comprehension, not of the universe but my place in it: how life is lived and perceived, how it can be ignored. Drunks take particular pleasure urinating against my small window, prison-like, momentarily flooding the glass with foamy liquid. It smells, can be unpleasant, but not without its peculiar comforts, even beauty: steaming gold liquid pelting the small window, in flooding or trickling streams.

A stepladder has helped me locate the strongest iron beam that bolts the roof to the walls and thus to the floor, onto which I secure a discarded electrical cord, strong enough to restrain an elephant. I knot it with patience and diligence, measure my neck once more, and let the noose dangle to eye level. Seen from my mattress, a sponge rats mistake for cheese, the noose looks harmless, even artistic. It is easy, all too easy: climb fifteen steps up the stepladder, ease my head into the noose, kick the ladder away: tonight, tomorrow, maybe in two weeks. All that kicking and choking, gasping, the struggle to breathe, to live, to exist. Maybe the noose is a reminder, a companion, a mute terror that enforces perspective, to live according to the strictest priorities of the soul. I nurse rat bites, on the toes, fingers, on my upper lip. Plague? What plague? I don't worry about such things any more: disease and things. What is a bubonic discomfort between friends?

PLEASURE

By the end of year one my sponge is all but eaten – rats determined to take the last comfort I thought I deserved. I sleep on a makeshift bed now, made from cardboard boxes that once contained television sets and refrigerators, from those tuberculosis awareness posters, from what remains of my tattered blankets. I have not lost my mind – not yet, though I cannot know what will come. A rat has severed my noose from the steel beam, thus putting into question my plan to be ready when the time comes. So the cord has now been replaced with a thin but strong wire immune to rat teeth. I cannot make up my mind, cannot decide whether – or when – to take that step, evoke total erasure. I am happy, smile alone in the dark, am in good health, but for the rat wounds that keep multiplying. I am being eaten alive, and though in pain, feel no pity for myself, no anger towards the furry little devils that cannot wait for me to fall asleep.

It *is* possible, I grin to myself in the dark, to reject the world! How triumphant that feeling is, complete ownership of one's time and life, walking west when every single living being is headed east. I have memories, reams and reams of them, some sharp and others faded. But I don't wallow in the past, a past that I have long left behind. How gratifying my insolence, how heartwarming my revolt against human wants that are so temporary and unremarkable, my living outside of time, indifferent to even the momentary nudges of manly lusts. How liberating living not knowing a Tuesday from an April, a minute after four to midday. How very profound life is in this cocoon, in the company of rats and my wire noose. I wonder to myself: how could Treblinka and Sorbibor have occurred on the same soil as Beethoven and Mozart? It makes no sense.

Then something happens. It drizzles. I hear car tyres splash water on a not-too-wet but not-dry tarmac. It is late, past midnight perhaps, when I'm awoken not by rats but by violent screams, the cries and thuds of a beating. I have heard screams before, but this is disturbing. A young woman wails: 'I give up. There is nothing I can do. Beat me, but don't kill me. You are going to hurt the child, Petrus, please mind the child. Beat me some other time; you are going to hurt the child. Can't we talk about this? I am begging and *praying* to you, my love. I told you, many times, I don't know that man. He comes to the shop, many times, but I don't know him. Ask the other girls. Are you going to kill me on the street like this, like a dog?'

But the blows and insults continue, so loud and so hard that the woman can cry no more, not even beg for her life to be spared. Only the baby cries between whatever blows he is raining on the mother, that penetrating cry of colic toddlers, a cry that shifts the heart. I think of the young Polish boy in my picture, a picture I keep under my pillow, thought how helpless *he* was, how brutal the world was for him.

I, very leisurely, reach for what remains of the wire, two metres of it maybe, and slowly make my way out onto the street. A scrawny man is sitting on a visibly pregnant young woman of not more than thirty, pounding her face with what looks like the spindle of a wooden chair. The baby has been flung from where Petrus wrestles and assaults its mother, landing in rainwater that speeds along the pavement and down into the drains below. It has stopped crying, smiles the moment I peer into its eyes, blinking under the streetlight. I kneel, make baby faces, smiling, grinning, blowing my cheeks like a cartoon character, all the while knotting a noose. To the end of the wire I attach a twig I have picked on my approach, so as not to lose grip.

It all happens lightning fast: by the time the man realises I am standing behind him, expressionless, he has been flung against the wall with such force as to knock out all his front teeth. He tries valiantly to fend me off with the spindle or chair leg he has been using against the woman's skull, but I am too quick, swift in my intentions. The second kick is so well aimed that I hear him groan, 'My testicles … Oh, good God, please take me now.' Only God isn't interested. He does not see that noose coming either, the force with which it is pulled so strong that it severs an artery in his neck, sending a spurt of blood up in the air and across the wall. He struggles, twists and turns, wide-eyed, fearful, until he is still, lifeless. I turn my gaze to the young woman, bruised and shivering; I nod, then return to my nest, to be eaten alive by rats, one small wound at a time.

I wake up in a hospital – one of those state ones full of advanced diseases and indifference – handcuffed to a bed. Two policemen stand guard on either side, bored stiff, one glancing at his wristwatch every two minutes. Apart from evident high fever (sweating, headache, double vision) and pain from new rat bites, I cannot say I am the unhappiest man I know. There are normal hospital routines and procedures: tablets, four hourly, an injection a day, and a drip with a solution that looks like urine. They refer to me as The Rat-Eaten Man In Bed 4, the young nurses, whom the impatient policemen corrects, saying that they should forget about the rats, and worry more about the Murderer In Bed 4. I am calm, in good spirits, having resolved many months back not to say a single word to anyone about anything; just to nod, and even then, only under extreme circumstances: to give voice to such turbulent emotional compulsion that silence cannot contain.

My hospital stay is hazy and I spend much of my time in some kind of delirium, but it does not escape me that the nurses are beautiful, even though I am cheated of their touch by their latex gloves. A doctor sees me shortly after midday on the second day, asks who can't or refuses to speak, and the short nurse, the one with big buttocks, points to Bed 4. He says he is Dr Cohen and, gloved and with the aid of some wooden ice-cream spoon, wants to check deep inside my mouth, 'To check what is going on in there.' I obey his every request, even though I know he will find nothing dramatic, beyond what God has placed there: teeth and tongue. He does, though, judging by a sudden, repulsed frown, find something that is to be expected, something that comes with being mute for months on end: foul breath. Dr Cohen asks me how I am feeling. I look at him vacantly, right through him, though not without a pleasant and vulnerable smile.

I eat well, a policemen secures my feet in leg irons when I have to use the toilet, stands guard at the door with his hand on his pistol. I wonder: when did I become so dangerous? The nurses bring me a form to fill, a form to rate the hospital menu, which I gently push aside. I do, however, notice one thing: the hospital name and address, which confirms to me that I am still in Cape Town. The wall clock says it is 2 pm: but what does that even mean, 2 pm? What difference does it make in the workings of the conscience and the universe? It might have been 2 am, and I would still not say a word, not even a grunt, not a nod to anything or anyone. Rats have eaten holes into my leather pants too, exposing little islands of my hairy thigh that contrast with the pitch-black leather that I think to be very beautiful and artistic.

I am released four nights later, with no name in my hospital file; frog-marched in leg irons to a police vehicle parked in a demarcated ambulance zone. Talk of breaking the law, procedure... I am driven to a penitentiary, marvel at the expansive sea, the beautiful sea dotted with ships, calm and majestic, like a giant sheet of blue glass spanning the coast.

I must have fallen asleep along the way, because I am rudely awoken by a dig in the ribs from the potbellied policeman with ashy elbows. He doesn't support, but drags me out of the vehicle and guides me, like one directs a horse or donkey, into the charge office. The president and his police top brass look down on me from pictures mounted on the walls, two juveniles are handcuffed together as if in a forced marriage, and police officers go through their routines: drinking tea, taking statements from aggrieved victims and perpetrators, restraining violent criminals. I am brought before a kind-hearted policewoman. I can smell kindness from forty miles away, sense it. After a long description of my mute tendencies by the arresting officers, she asks for my names or any form of identification. I look at her with fondness and reverence, but maintain silence. I am then fingerprinted, without latex gloves, and escorted to a side room where I am handcuffed to a table. They ask me a string of boring and tedious questions, but I doze off, probably because the rats have been keeping me awake for months now, robbing me of restful sleep. A youngish policemen bearing papers walks into the room, wide-eyed.

'The database says he is one Milton Mohlele, but Mohlele is dead. Has been for over two years now. We checked with Home Affairs, and they too confirm he is or should be dead. Hospital reports, death certificates, pathology reports are all here.' He waves the wad of papers and sets them down in front of his superior. 'Everything checks out.'

'Well,' says the commanding officer, whose name badge reads Bernard Mazibuko, chewing gum, 'Mr Mohlele is clearly not dead. He is right here next to me, handcuffed to a table. I can smell his breath from a thousand miles. A little eaten by rats, as you people say, but very much alive. Charge him with first-degree murder and one count of fraud. Check what the statute says about people who fake deaths and charge him with that too. Investigate everything: drugs, insurance fraud, liaisons with hookers, other murders, gang activity, money laundering, syndicates of whatever kind – and then nail this dead man to the wall for me, will you?'

A second officer storms in, also with a batch of papers. 'He is famous,' she says. 'An acclaimed writer.'

'Famous writer, *my voet*. Where have you ever seen any acclaimed anybody in anything eaten by rats? Have you lost your mind, De Klerk?'

'No, sir.'

'What do you people think this is? A game? First you tell me he is dead, now he is suddenly a famous writer. What are you going to tell me next, that he is Leonardo da Vinci? I don't have time for nonsense. Unshackle this mute, horrid-breath, famous, rat-eaten dead man of yours and lock him up. End of story.'

Unless you are an eternal optimist, prison – by its very nature and design – is not a pleasant place. And yet I am happy here, content, locked into a single holding cell. Reasons advanced, talk I overhear, is that I am a flight risk and on suicide watch. I have no such thoughts at present, and in fact, have not felt so alive in a very long time. Apart from aches and itches from rat bites, I do not have any other discomfort other than a fast-subsiding fever. Mazibuko offers me stringent conditions for bail, enquires what arrangements I have in place for an attorney. I look at him with kindness and understanding, with empathy, but do not utter a single word.

Three policemen came to my cell last night, kicked and slapped me around. 'You are not fooling us, you swine. We know you can talk. How did you teach at the Culture Institute if you're mute – tell us that? And those television appearances? Speak! D'you suddenly, conveniently, have cucumbers growing out of your fucking throat? You think we stupid?' They call me names, all sorts of names. I am not upset; I hold no grudges against any of them. They don't understand. This is why I am so patient with all of them, with how tackily they treat me. Murder? What happened was not murder. Apart from temporary disregard of the Sixth Commandment, I think of it as ... well, as the results of a provoked conscience. That has a sweet ring to it, and explains, to me at least, that there are exceptions when it comes to human life. That life is sacred is not in dispute, but what does one do when one's conscience is so violated, so callously provoked? How could that possibly be murder?

Three weeks pass. My court appearance, during which I am asked to plead, is over almost as soon as it starts. Eleven minutes, at the most. I agree, with a slight nod, to one thing and one thing only: that it is true that I am responsible for the death of a man I come to know as Petrus Hendricks, 44, the son of a reverend and owner of one or two struggling supermarkets, reformed car thief and first-year and part-time student in Criminology. The primary witness is Beulah Hendricks, 28, his wife of seven years, who looks at me with fondness and admiration. What beautiful dimples she has, what lovely hands, what a sweet, sweet voice. What a pure heart.

So they were driving through the factory area, from a family business, headed to Rondebosch, arguing about what Mr Hendricks suggested was a secret lover, when the Opel Astra broke down, and the argument worsened. That is where I entered their story. They could not have possibly known that there was a man with a reliable wire being eaten by rats in a basement room just metres away; and I, on the other hand, couldn't have planned that my conscience would be so perturbed, so disdained, so violated that the only solution to the problem was the unfortunate but deserved early grave for Mr Hendricks.

I don't think about Petrus at all, a little about Beulah (but not too much), and within selected pockets of time, maybe a thought or two about myself. I overhear that newspapers are churning unbelievable profits, that airwaves are abuzz with all sorts of commentary, that my matter has duly been dubbed The Ghost Trial. Mazibuko urges me to consider bail, says that on second thought, on closer consideration of my docket, there seems to be no grounds to deny me bail, as long as I can provide a reliable address. I look at him with gratitude, but do not say a word or even gesture my agreement or opposition; something that frustrates him greatly. The truth is: I am not uncomfortable in jail. My lodgings at the abandoned printing works are worse, in fact, less than ideal. All this talk about bail: for what?

I am back in court three weeks later: the state has completed its investigation in relation to the murder charge, and believe – a sentiment I agree with wholeheartedly – that it has a strong and winnable case against me. There is the bloodied noose, my more-than-clear fingerprint on an old chair leg Petrus used to try to fend me off, they have Beulah's sworn statement recorded not in malice but in service of the truth, and finally, my signature agreeing to the obvious but not the philosophical complexities of the murder charge. How inadequate the rituals of humans, how short-sighted, how rigid!

They are all here: an elderly judge who looks like a famous orchestra conductor, a spiteful and arrogant state prosecutor, the attorney the state has imposed on me, old friends and mild enemies, newspaper and television people, court assistants, police on guard, gossipmongers, and that faceless throng referred to as 'the general public'. I, as much as I don't fancy talking, don't expect or wish that the trial be long or cumbersome. I have admitted, registered no objections of any kind, and await judgement and sentencing. Why complicate such a straightforward matter with sketches, exhibits, pathology reports and the one hundred and forty-six pictures taken at the crime scene, adjournments, recesses, specialists explaining with the aid of computer-generated infographics the process and phases of death by strangulation, and pontifications about premeditation and my mental health? It is all unnecessarily thorough – too detailed for a man who has not denied anything, whose attitude has always been: give me anything linking me to the crime and I will sign it in a heartbeat. But don't ask me to talk and explain anything … I have nothing to say, nothing that would be understood, anyway.

Back in incarceration – though I still do not utter a single word, not even a nod this time – I derive great pleasure from a surprise visit from one Beulah Hendricks. The bruises have faded, some completely gone. She is reserved but cheerful, and has brought with her what must be the most beautiful baby in Cape Town. It is as if the baby recognises me, knows me, and an eagerness in his face suggests he has something urgent to tell me: something lost in drool and baby mumble.

What a relief it is to be out of the leg irons, but also to be barricaded from the outside world by glass and grid gates. It is not a long visit. She has brought me chicken curry and steamed vegetables, some fruit, and a selection of carefully chosen toiletries not for Paris ramps – but not for factory floors either. Modest brands on a modest budget. She looks at me with emotion, one I can't quite place, her smile quivering, her eyes watering, and the love with which she describes the contents of the food parcels, how they were prepared with what ingredients for what culinary effect, almost draws words out of me. I am deeply touched – mainly by the contradiction that my hands had robbed her of a husband, but that her heart seems to think otherwise.

The food keeps coming with each subsequent visit: roast beef, pasta, more toiletries, fruit, and one day … a picture of a group of schoolgirls. I recognise her instantly as the beauty in the second row, head tilted to the side, resting on a violin. I point, prompting her to break into a grin, to blush. She has for the previous visits, twenty-three in total, dressed rather conservatively, but she is on this particular visit in a floral dress that is neither too reserved nor too revealing: it has a way of hugging her figure and illuminating her complexion, and combined with those low-hanging earrings made from peacock feathers and a matching handbag, Beulah Hendricks is a sight to behold. And she smells good, not those perfumes that scream at you from the top of Everest, but a fresh and understated scent that is there without really being there, that blends into everything and nothingness. I admit to being taken by that dress, to my thoughts wandering not into realms of the perverse, but to imagining how those buds at the tips of her adequate breasts feel to touch, how they would respond if one struck them like a guitarist's thumbs touch and pull away from strings, like one lightly or ferociously plucks on harp strings. She senses my thoughts, that's for sure – women are sensitive to these things – because she leans forward, closer to the glass barricade separating us, and with her thumb and index finger, separates the front slit of her dress, discreetly revealing one real and one dummy breast.

'The left one had to go. Amputation. A mastectomy. A lump and all the horrors that go with it. The other one is healthy, but I cannot show it to you. I fear I would be embarrassed, that it would be inappropriate. You know, me oozing milk and all.' That catches me off guard. Perhaps I even smile, for she promptly follows with, 'Excuse me, I have to go. I left David with my mom. He cries a lot if I am not home.' I nod: so purified by desire, a certain new pleasure – pleasure with comprehension.

If you ever wanted to hear anything profound, anything worth remembering, something precise and trimmed of worthless speculations, you must hear it from the last wishes of the dying. From those ruined by disease, fatally wounded or facing a firing squad. It is only then that lucidity enters a life, that life is stripped of all excesses and pretences, that its true value reveals itself. One realises, only then, when the rituals of dying have been initiated that we understand that life is one long preparation for the manner and outcome of death.

It is only those who have surrendered all, scoured the very depths of consciousness, who will understand a controversial notion: that all of life's greatest pleasures are smokescreens, since none ever truly lasts and, if it does, it is so encumbered with boredom and routine as to not be pleasure at all. Affairs exist because marital copulation and friendships become stale and dreary; spasms of faith and the spiritual fade because some heavenly answers never come; and the innocence of children is false because none of them knows who they are and how to express themselves. Some grow to develop an addiction for gluttony, be trusted doctors who inject the elderly with swimming-pool chemicals. This thing called and known and experienced as *pleasure* is a trick to fool the mind that whole lifetimes must be committed to courting and securing pleasures that don't exist. How oppressive the ways of pleasure, how hopelessly inadequate their routines, that even the problems that supposedly engulf love are yet to be understood, perfected. The truest and greatest pleasures, therefore, exist not between people and things, but lurk in the tiniest fragments of a moment, the unlikeliest encounters and the most improbable of outcomes, entirely unrelated scenarios fusing into concoctions of meaning.

The Dreamer on the Prison Floor

I dream, not as Giovanni Gomez, but as Milton, as me: in black and white, as if observing a giant screen, watching an old documentary film unfold, with less-than-perfect pictures. Everything in the dream is old, 1940s' old: the bicycles, the bridges, and the dresses the women wear. The Führer is not dead. I see him, show him a rude finger, but he does not seem to see me. Or maybe he just doesn't care. He is weeping for Eva Braun. She has left him, because he is sick and unpleasant, because he has lost his powers of war and oratory. No one salutes him any more. I can see from his face that he feels betrayed, that he is pained, in shock. That hand of his shakes badly, so badly that even children see it; they mock him, imitate his tremors in their games, act out the once-powerful Führer becoming of slurred speech, a cripple before their very eyes.

Berlin is not in ruins. Not a single building has been bombed. All the bombs dropped have been betrayed by gravity. They hover around like metal balloons over German skies, all these bombs floating over Germany intended for its destruction. They float in chaotic formation, casting moving shadows across the streets below. There are so many bombs that they almost block the sun, rob it of its majesty, reducing it to pitiful candle flames. A train stands idle on rusty rails – a long train, with rusty wheels and wooden carriages on which a child has scrawled in chalk, skew wording: *One Stop Nuremberg*. No one pays any attention to the bombs. We have too much faith in gravity, faith that the bombs won't fall earthwards, obliterate our cities. Gravity has decided to switch sides, has tired of pulling and dropping things to earth. So many bombs suspended in mid-air – so few flowers, beautiful birds, so few mirrors.

Hangman's scaffolds have been erected along the railway line – hundreds of them – poles from which uniformed SS men hang by their bootstraps, their ankles bound by wire, wire that cuts into their flesh and into bone. Like pendulums they swing, some groaning in pain, some beaten and bloodied, others simply stiffened corpses whose eyes have been gouged out, whose teeth have been hammered out with a blunt object. Flies buzz around them, on them, creep into their hollow and greasy eye sockets, crawling with maggots and caked blood. There are also famous faces: Rudolf Hess, Martin Bormann and Wilhelm Frick and the others, covered in flies from their bowel mishaps. A rabbi stands on a makeshift podium – planks nailed to a tin drum – silently mumbling words from the Torah. It is not last rites – not exactly – but something similar. Because of the stench, the rabbi leans on one of the drums, out of breath, a handkerchief tightly held to his nose, and with considered wailing not without dignity and composure, kneels and kisses the dusty ground.

I wake drenched in sweat, thirstier than I have ever been and wonder: who carried out those beatings?

It is impossible to empty the mind of everything for it wanders in the most sudden and unexpected ways, and brings with it pangs of longing. What have Orapeleng, Alexis and Abella read in the newspapers about me? Do they believe the deep-vein thrombosis? Has my accomplice, if my beloveds became suspicious, covered our tracks well with convincing medical records and pathology reports to convince even the most sceptic that I am indeed dead and cremated, not burrowing in some factory dungeon, staring at darkness?

I have not uttered a single word in months; except for the occasional yawn, my jaws seem wired shut. A thought occupies all of my being: what has become of the young boy dragging a damaged kite along a street in Poland? This thought, the memory of that picture, fills my existence in ways I cannot explain: how small and helpless he was, surrounded by smouldering ruins and the Führer's army. I remember that picture well, see it in the darkness: how he clasped both his elbows, head leaning forwards, frozen to the core. Did he grow to discover pleasures of the universe, was he one of the lucky ones, or was he obliterated and buried under rubble by the Führer's bombs? How cheerful his eyes were, startled only by the marching army.

Or maybe I read the eclipse of sorrow in those eyes, distress over the broken kite, a kite that had nowhere to fly because Polish skies were raining bombs. I am tempted to call him pretty for he was more than handsome: that smallish mouth and those beady eyes, those fragile knees of his, those hands concerned only with the survival and flight of kites, his indifference to the marching army. How adorable, how amusing, how touching his shoes, worn wrong, right shoe swapped with the left, that acceptance of discomfort, while his thoughts hovered elsewhere. I wonder what I would name him if he were mine, a name that would do that photograph justice – an inviting but dignified name, one to free all skies of bombs, to set free a trillion kites.

Acknowledgements

I would like to acknowledge my once girlfriend, and now wife, Sharon Mohlele, for letting me be; for allowing me to write in bed during what was supposed to be family and private time.

Mr Steven Spielberg, for the impact *Schindler's List* has had on the emotional thrust of this book. Martin Amis' *Time's Arrow* has also been invaluable in the creative reimagining and expression of horror.

I am indebted, too, to my friend of decades and counting, Malose Lekganyane, who has a God-given ability to explain complex moral dilemmas of the general and particular kind: Kgomo, Mohwaduba!

Pleasure would not have been possible without the evocative music of Simphiwe Dana, Nina Simone and Carlos Santana – amongst others. I note and act on the moral impossibility of being grateful to the Third Reich for keeping such meticulous records of Second World War Germany and the Hitler years.

I extend my gratitude, too, to my very able and passionate

editor Sean Fraser; Andrea Nattrass, my diligent and persuasive publisher; elder Bra Mandla Langa and mentor Professor Keorapetse Kgositsile for listening to me dream this book; Thando Mgqolozana for those literary therapy phone calls; Zukiswa Wanner for those inspired WhatsApps.

There is, of course, Paige Nick, a writer's writer; Wits University's Dan Ojwang, a teacher and a friend; Professor Dineo Gqola, who makes it so much easier to create intelligent women characters; Phakama Mbonambi's long, expensive phone calls in the service of literature; the friendship of Wesley Peter and Sis Tiny Dolamo; the laughter of Commissioner Terry Tselane; my uncles Brown Mohlele and Mabulana Mohlele; the laughter and friendship of Patrick Monkoe; the sober mind of my brother Jeffrey Mohlele; and the critical lessons in thinking and manhood taught to me by my late uncle Malekutu Mohlele.

I am eternally indebted to former South African president, His Excellency Thabo Mbeki, for his 'I am an African' speech.